Tom hadn't seen a woman blush in years. It looked good on her.

"And what do you do best?" Callie asked.

"I don't know anymore. I used to be a damn good marine."

"And what else are you good at?"

Callie's words surprised him. So did her attitude. She wasn't avoiding his gaze, wasn't staring at him with pity. "Football," he replied. "I was good at football. And playing the accordion." He felt like an idiot for revealing that top secret bit of intel. "And kissing."

"Naturally. All marines who are good at football and the accordion are good at kissing."

Now she was mocking him. To his surprise, he liked it.

Dear Reader,

No month better suits Silhouette Romance than February. For it celebrates that breathless feeling of first love, the priceless experiences and memories that come with a longtime love and the many hopes and dreams that give a couple's life together so much meaning. At Silhouette Romance, our writers try to capture all these feelings in their timeless tales…and this month's lineup is no exception.

Our PERPETUALLY YOURS promotion continues this month with a charming tale from Sandra Paul. In *Domesticating Luc* (#1802) a dog trainer gets more than she bargained for when she takes on an unruly puppy and his very obstinate and irresistible owner. Beloved author Judy Christenberry returns to the lineup with *Honeymoon Hunt* (#1803)—a madcap adventure in which two opposites pair up to find their parents who have eloped, but instead wind up on a tight race to the finish line, er, altar! In *A Dash of Romance* (#1804) Elizabeth Harbison creates the perfect recipe for love when she pairs a self-made billionaire with a spirited waitress. Cathie Linz rounds out the offerings with *Lone Star Marine* (#1805). Part of her MEN OF HONOR series, this poignant romance features a wounded soldier who craves only the solitude to heal, and finds that his lively and beautiful neighbor just might be the key to the future he hadn't dreamed possible.

As always, be sure to return next month when Alice Sharpe concludes our PERPETUALLY YOURS promotion.

Happy reading.

Ann Leslie Tuttle
Associate Senior Editor

Please address questions and book requests to:
Silhouette Reader Service
U.S.: 3010 Walden Ave., P.O. Box 1325, Buffalo, NY 14269
Canadian: P.O. Box 609, Fort Erie, Ont. L2A 5X3

LONE STAR MARINE

CATHIE LINZ

SILHOUETTE *Romance*®

Published by Silhouette Books

America's Publisher of Contemporary Romance

For anyone who has ever been bullied.
Special thanks to all you readers who have
enjoyed my Men of Honor series!

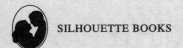 SILHOUETTE BOOKS

ISBN 0-373-19805-1

LONE STAR MARINE

Copyright © 2006 by Cathie L. Baumgardner

This edition published by arrangement with Harlequin Books S.A.

® and TM are trademarks of Harlequin Books S.A., used under license.
Trademarks indicated with ® are registered in the United States Patent
and Trademark Office, the Canadian Trade Marks Office and in other
countries.

Visit Silhouette Books at www.eHarlequin.com

Printed in U.S.A.

CATHIE LINZ

left her career in a university law library to become a *USA TODAY* bestselling author of contemporary romances. She is the recipient of the highly coveted Storyteller of the Year Award given by *Romantic Times BOOKclub* and has been nominated for a Love and Laughter Career Achievement Award for the delightful humor in her books.

Although Cathie loves to travel, she is always glad to get back home to her family, her various cats, her trusty computer and her hidden cache of Oreo cookies!

Dear Reader,

There's just something about a guy in uniform...especially a dress blues uniform! I first got the idea for my Men of Honor series when Sergeant Major Robin White came to speak at my Windy City writers group. As he talked about honor, courage and commitment, I realized that these are all traits that a real hero should have.

The more I researched the marines the more I appreciated their unique strengths. *Semper fi*—always faithful—isn't just a saying, it's a way of life for the men and women who sign up to join the Corps.

And so it is with much gratitude that I salute all the Marines who have so bravely served their country, as well as those who continue to serve. And to all their families who have stood beside them, keeping the home fires burning. You're all heroes to me.

Semper fi,

Cathie Linz

Chapter One

Tom Kozlowski heard the knock on the cabin door and decided to ignore it. He was on disability leave from his beloved Marine Corps, so he didn't have to obey orders of any kind. He'd come to the family's King Ranch outside of San Antonio to get away from people staring at him with looks of pity, with smiles of false hope.

A second knock followed the first.

Tom continued to disregard it.

The third knock had a definite edge to it and was followed by what could only be described as downright pounding.

Totally aggravated now, Tom yanked the door open. "What?" he growled.

"Oh good!" a peppy, feminine voice said. "I'm so glad you're here."

He blinked at the sexy vision standing there. She was wearing jeans that accentuated her great body and a tank top beneath a denim jacket. Her hair was red and her lips sinful.

"What do you want?"

"Your brother Striker sent me." She smiled at him and confidently stepped inside.

Tom had to grip the door frame to keep his balance as he turned to watch her.

He'd just talked to Striker a short while ago on his cellphone. Striker hadn't said anything about sending a visitor out to see him.

Was this female supposed to be a surprise? Like the last surprise Striker had sent him: a strippergram.

Tom had been clueless then, but now he knew the routine. "Striker sent you, huh?"

"That's right."

"Do you have a name?"

"Callie."

"Well, Callie, would you like me to take your jacket?"

"Oh, well, I guess it is a little warm in here…."

He watched her remove her denim jacket, then took it from her to drop on a nearby chair. She looked a little awkward, as if she was unsure what to do next.

Wanting to put her at ease, he said, "I know the routine. You can cut to the chase."

"I can?"

He nodded. "Absolutely."

"I know your time is valuable—"

"So is yours."

She shot him a big smile, one that hit him with the force of a hand grenade. What was going on here? He felt a sense of recognition that caught him totally by surprise, yet he was sure he hadn't met her before. He tried to focus on the words coming from her lovely mouth.

"Thanks so much for saying that. I don't know what Striker has told you about me…"

"Not much."

"Well, people in my line of work are often misunderstood."

"I imagine so." What he was really imagining was her slipping her hands beneath the hem of her tank top and slowly sliding it up over her head. Was she really a stripper? Why else would she say that people in her line of work are misunderstood?

"They don't take us seriously," she added.

"I won't make that mistake," he noted, wondering if maybe she was a college student or someone trying to work her way through graduate school.

"That's so sweet of you. You know, even though we've just met, I feel like I already know you."

"Yes, I feel that way, too." The last stripper had rubbed her hands all over him and he hadn't reacted at all. But Tom only had to look at Callie and he was shaken to his core.

"A lot of people don't consider what I do to be really teaching."

"I'm sure this encounter will be very educational," he reassured her before cupping one hand on her shoulder and drawing her closer. He had to keep one hand on the cane that kept him from falling on his face. As it was, she sort of stumbled against him, making him lose his balance and resulting in them both falling onto the couch.

"I'm so sorry!" She scrambled off him, making him groan. "Did I hurt you?" She leaned closer to study his face.

This was his chance and he took it. His mouth barely touched hers when she shoved him away.

"Hey!" She stood glaring down at him like some kind of enraged goddess. "What do you think you're doing?"

"Kissing…you." Tom was having a difficult time forming words.

"Are you drunk?"

"No." He couldn't have alcohol with the medication he was taking. His fuzzy brain was a result of being so close to Callie. There was something about her that prevented him from thinking straight. It wasn't just her looks. He'd seen beautiful women before. It was *her,* which made him very uneasy.

Some of the men in his family had a habit of falling in love at first sight, even if it took them a while to admit it. He certainly didn't want that fate to befall him. Not when he had nothing to offer a woman.

"What made you think you had a right to kiss me?" Callie demanded.

Okay, truth was, he was no expert on situations like this and he hated feeling like an idiot. "Do I have to pay more for kisses? If so, that's fine. Just tell me how much."

"*Pay?*" she sputtered, her face turning red with anger. "There isn't enough money in the entire state of Texas."

"Listen, you don't have to get on your high horse with me. You're the one who came knocking on *my* door."

"Because your brother Striker sent me."

"Yes, he sent the last stripper, too."

"What?!"

Tom winced at the loud volume of her shriek.

"I am *not* a stripper!" She grabbed her denim jacket and yanked it around her body as if to protect herself from him.

"Then why are you here?"

"To pick up the key to the North Cabin. Striker told me you had it."

Tom frowned, trying to make sense of her words. "Why do you need the key?"

"Because I've rented the cabin for the summer."

Callie could tell that Tom was not pleased with this news. Well, too bad. She wasn't pleased at him mistaking her for a stripper.

And to think she'd actually been attracted to him when he'd first opened the door. There had been more than just physical awareness, though.

She felt as if she already knew him, but that must be because she'd heard so much about him over the years—about what an honorable, by-the-book officer he was in the Marine Corps.

Most recently, Striker had told her about his youngest brother's injuries and the three operations it had taken to put Tom's leg back together again.

She'd seen the earlier photos of him in his dress blues, his dark hair in a short military cut.

Tom looked different now. Like a dark angel fallen from grace. His hair was longer, his face gaunt. There was a scar on his right cheek. He looked tough.

But it was his eyes that got to her. They held the shadows of a man who'd seen more than his fair share of pain and suffering—a wounded warrior.

He wore dark sweatpants and a dark T-shirt with the sleeves ripped off that allowed her to see how muscular his arms were. Even though he was leaning on a cane, he possessed an incredibly powerful presence that made her feel all fluttery inside.

She wasn't the kind to lust after a sexy Marine. Something else—something *more*—was going on here.

She'd experienced an incredibly strong emotional pull toward him sensing there was more to him than she could see on the surface.

"The North Cabin is only a few hundred yards from this cabin," Tom said.

"I know."

"You can't stay there. There must be some mistake."

"I'll say. A *big* mistake, you thinking I was some kind of stripper."

"You're the one who said that people in your line of work are often misunderstood and not taken seriously."

"I was talking about my work as a kindergarten teacher."

She didn't look like any kindergarten teacher he'd ever seen. Weren't they supposed to be kindly and asexual?

"Call your brother and check it out with him if you don't believe me."

Now she was making him feel stupid for having jumped to conclusions about her, which ticked him off. "I plan on doing just that."

"Go right ahead."

Striker answered on the second ring. "Who is this woman you sent up here?" Tom demanded.

"Callie? She's rented the North Cabin for the summer. I told her to stop by your cabin to pick up the key."

"Nice of you to let me know ahead of time," Tom growled.

"Is there a problem?"

"Yes, I didn't realize I'd have a neighbor."

"Don't blame Callie. And be polite to her. She's Tex's granddaughter."

"Tex?"

"My executive assistant."

"That would be me," an older woman announced in a grouchy voice from the doorway. She was just a little bitty thing, but she had the bearing of a general as she marched across the room to glare at him. "The door wasn't latched, so I came on in to see what was going on in here and why it was taking so long to get a simple key."

"Mr. Kozlowski wasn't expecting me," Callie said.

That was putting it mildly. "*Captain* Kozlowski," Tom curtly corrected her.

"Now don't go getting all Marine-like on me," Tex said. "That dog just ain't gonna hunt."

"Is that Tex I hear in the background?" Striker demanded.

"Affirmative."

"Put her on the phone."

"Striker wants to talk to you." Tom handed the phone over and awkwardly stepped away.

While Tex was momentarily distracted by her conversation with her boss, Callie approached Tom and spoke in a low voice. "Don't tell my grandmother that you thought I was a stripper."

Like he was on the verge of doing something stupid like that.

"It would upset her."

He hadn't felt too good about it, either.

"I apologize for the misunderstanding." His voice sounded as stiff as he felt.

"I had no idea you were expecting…someone like that."

She made it sound like he made a habit of having strippers come to his door. "I wasn't expecting anyone."

"No? Do you usually assume that every female who knocks on your door is a…you know." She clearly didn't want to say the word in case her grandmother overheard.

"Of course not."

"So it was me then?" Now her voice was mocking. "Something about the wild way I was dressed?" She pointed to her ordinary jeans, tank top and denim jacket. "I'd really like to know so no other guy makes the same mistake you did."

"Very funny." His growl didn't sound as fierce as he'd hoped.

"Are you okay?" She studied him closely. "You look a little pale."

"I just need some peace and quiet." *And a bionic body.* His knee felt as if Godzilla and King Kong had both stomped on it. Several times.

That's what he got for trying to run before he could walk. Literally. He'd wanted to take a run. So he had. Or tried to. Hadn't gotten very far, though.

Sure, the physical therapists at the San Antonio military medical facility, where he underwent rehab every day, had warned him about overdoing it.

But he was a Marine. Pain was merely weakness leaving his body.

"You need some peace and quiet? Fine." She stepped away from him. "Give me the key and we'll be out of here faster than a prairie fire with a tailwind."

He pointed to a hook near the door. "There's the key."

"Striker wants to talk to you," Tex said, handing the phone back to him. "Welcome to Texas."

Tom waited until the two women had left the cabin before he sank into the couch, grimacing as the burning, knifelike twinges grew to an angry throb in his right knee. He took his aggravation out on his oldest brother. "Why did you rent out the North Cabin? You know I came here to get away from people."

"Callie isn't people. She's practically family."

"Trust me, I didn't feel at all familial toward her." Tom still didn't know how to describe what had happened when his lips had touched hers, but it was something monumental.

And he couldn't do monumental.

Not now.

Not when his entire future was up in the air, when he didn't even know who he was anymore or what his purpose in life was.

"You didn't do anything stupid, did you?" Striker demanded.

"You mean, like think she was a stripper?"

Striker groaned. "Tell me you didn't...."

"Oh, but I did." Tom closed his eyes and rubbed his hand over his aching knee.

"Did she know?"

"That I thought she was a stripper? Affirmative."

"Why would you think that?"

"Because the last female you sent out here was a stripper."

"Yeah, but Callie—"

"Is a very beautiful woman. And she said some stuff that made me believe she was in that line of work."

"But she's a kindergarten teacher."

"Well, how was I supposed to know that?"

"By asking her."

"Forgive me if I wasn't in the mood for conversation."

Over the phone, Tom heard a muffled voice in the background before Striker said, "Kate wants to know if you took your pain medication today."

Kate was Striker's wife, an attorney and a Texas girl from a wealthy neighboring ranch. They had a three-year-old son, Sean, and Kate was eight months pregnant with their second child. She'd been hovering over Tom since he'd arrived at the ranch.

"Or are you still being stupid and stubborn about it?" Striker added.

"I doubt she put it that way."

"Okay, so I rephrased the question. Answer it."

Tom bristled at the bossy tone of Striker's voice. His oldest brother didn't seem able to accept the fact that Tom was an adult.

Tom wondered if he'd made a mistake by coming here. He'd had the choice of the ranch or Striker's beach house on Pirate's Cove, an island off the coast of North Carolina. Or even his parents' home in Chicago.

Maybe he should have avoided his family altogether.

"Striker, be nice." Tom heard Kate's reprimand of her husband before taking the phone from him. "Hey, Tom, how's it going?"

"How do you live with him?" Tom demanded.

Kate laughed. "I've had a crush on him since I was seventeen."

"That explains it then."

"So how are you doing?"

"Just peachy."

"You took your medication?" She sounded concerned.

"I will."

"I know you hate taking it, but it's the best way to help your body heal."

Tom wasn't sure he'd ever heal. And he hated that weakness. He was a Marine, a breed apart, trained to conform to an uncompromising code of honor, courage and discipline.

He was tough and battle hardened.

He had brash courage in the face of long odds.

Besides, plenty of his fellow Marines had it much worse than he did.

"Tom, call if you need anything, okay?" Kate added.

"Affirmative." But his sister-in-law couldn't provide what Tom needed. No one could. Because he needed to feel whole again, and deep down inside he was starting to doubt that day would ever come.

"Whooee," Tex exclaimed as Callie opened the door of the North Cabin. "That baby brother of Striker's is a mighty good-looking one."

"Is he? I hadn't noticed."

"And if I believed that, I'd have the IQ of a cantaloupe. You think I didn't notice the tension between you two? What went on in there?"

"Nothing."

It was silly and emotionally very risky to form a connection with a man she'd just met. Especially one who was not pleased at having her rent this cabin.

Callie didn't realize she'd spoken her last words aloud until Tex said, "What do you mean he's not pleased?" Her grandmother placed her hands on her hips as if she was ready to do battle. "Why not? He thinks you're not good enough to be staying here?"

"No, not at all. I don't think he wants *anyone* staying here. I got the impression that he really wants to be alone."

"Him and Greta Garbo. Where do you want this box?"

"That's too heavy for you to be lifting." Callie tried to take it from her grandmother, but Tex refused to let it go.

Instead, she narrowed her blue eyes at her. "Are you saying I'm old?"

"Of course not." Callie knew better than to enter that discussion. Tex was really sensitive when it came to her age.

"Then just tell me where this goes."

"The kitchen."

Callie had put most of her things in storage and had only brought the minimum, enough to manage for the three months until her new town house was completed. Bad weather had delayed its construction. The original plan was that the town house would be ready when her lease ran out.

But things hadn't worked out that way. When Tex mentioned Callie's problem to Striker, he'd immediately offered the empty cabin.

Normally, Callie wouldn't have taken advantage of it, but she'd run out of options. Her dad, a sales rep for a tool company, had been recently transferred to Dallas, so she couldn't stay with him. Since her mom had died in a fire when Callie was ten, her dad had raised her single-handedly. He'd always made her feel that she was his shining star and that he was there for her, even when he traveled and she stayed with her grandmother Tex.

She doubted that her father would be understanding of Tom briefly mistaking her for a stripper.

But Callie wasn't holding a grudge.

Because, despite having a loving family, Callie knew what it was like to feel totally alone and not want another living soul to know it. She'd seen that emotion flash in Tom's eyes for one brief moment tonight, and it had been like an arrow shot right through her heart.

Tom had another bad night.

He was used to them by now.

That didn't mean he liked them.

Or the dreams.

Nightmares really...reliving his patchwork memories of a red flash, the ringing in his ears, not being able to hear or move. Looking down and seeing his bloodied leg.

He really hated remembering those images.

Which was why he refused to even acknowledge that they occurred.

Instead, every morning, he wiped his mind clean like one of those Etch A Sketch toy drawing screens his niece, Amy, liked so much.

Amy was his brother Ben's daughter. Ben adopted her when he'd married Ellie. Tom had missed the wedding in North Carolina but had attended the renewal of their vows on their first anniversary.

Ellie was pregnant now. Last he'd heard, there was a betting pool going on in the Kozlowski family to see who would deliver first: Ellie or Kate. Both had due dates near the end of June.

Tom was the only remaining Kozlowski bachelor. Even his twin brother, Steve, had bitten the bullet and gotten hitched—to a librarian of all people. Not the type of woman Tom ever would have thought Steve would like, let alone love.

Marriage was not on Tom's agenda. As a Marine with money, the result of an inheritance from his oil-baron grandfather, Hank King, Tom had gotten plenty of attention from the female population.

Even after his injuries, a few of them had still come around. But he'd seen the look in their eyes. The revulsion. He'd sent them packing. Except for Penny. She'd gotten under his skin when he'd been at his most vulnerable: after learning he wouldn't be returning to command his unit and that someone else would be replacing him.

She'd comforted him. And then betrayed him.

She'd taught him a valuable lesson: vulnerability equals weakness.

Tom got out of bed and almost tripped over his dog, Arf, who was lying on the rug beside the bed. He still couldn't believe he actually had a dog. That hadn't been on his agenda, either. But somehow he'd ended up with the mutt.

Striker tried claiming that Arf was a poodle of some kind, but Tom refused to accept that. No way a tough Marine would be caught dead with a girlie poodle.

No, Arf was a mutt. A loyal one. A quiet one who didn't say much. Didn't bark much. Just looked at him with adoration. That worked for Tom.

"Breakfast at 0600 hours," he told the mutt. "Ready for your chow?"

First, Tom had to let Arf out to do his business. The dog was already at the front door.

"I'm coming, I'm coming." His inability to move with the speed he once had was just one of the many things he was having a hard time accepting.

"There." Tom threw open the door and stood there in his navy-blue boxer shorts while the dog raced outside.

Only then did it belatedly hit him that he wasn't the only one up at this early hour.

Arf was racing toward Callie, who had her backside to him.

"Watch out!" Tom yelled.

Callie turned to face him. He could see her eyes widen as she stared at him standing there in his underwear.

And he could see Arf taking a flying leap at Callie.

At first, Tom thought that his dog had knocked her over, but then he realized that she must have simply lost her balance because Arf wasn't big enough to dent a marshmallow.

It took him a moment or two to get to Callie, who was still sitting on the dusty ground, laughing as Arf licked her face.

"I'm sorry," Tom said. "Arf, get away from her, you idiot. Sit! No, not *on* her!"

Callie laughed. "I didn't know you had a dog."

"He barely qualifies as a dog sizewise."

"I didn't see him in your cabin yesterday."

"He was asleep. Nothing wakes him then. Come on, Arf. Sit!" The dog finally obeyed, sitting down and looking up at Tom expectantly.

"Let me help you up." Tom offered his free hand.

When she hesitated, he said, "I'm not so decrepit that I can't help you up."

Callie didn't think he was decrepit. She thought he was entirely too sexy first thing in the morning.

But she gave him her hand and he tugged her to her feet in one smooth motion. A little too smooth, because she ended up standing mere inches from his mostly bare body.

His shoulders were as wide as a tank, and there was a dark shadow of stubble on his austere face. He radiated heat.

She'd seen the multiple fading scars on his chest from shrapnel wounds. The scars on his right leg were fiercer and redder, a reminder of his most-recent surgery.

He'd almost died.

She'd almost never met him.

She hurt for him. She wanted to wave a magic wand over him and take all the pain away.

Not that she felt sorry for him. Far from it.

She was aware of every breath he took. Dazed by the unexpected shivers of pleasure dancing down her spine, she couldn't seem to look away from his gaze.

He had the most incredible eyes. They were a unique combination of light brown and green. Some people might describe them as hazel, but she'd seen hazel eyes before and they weren't as fascinating as his.

"Are you okay?" His voice was pretty incredible, too. Rich and rumbly.

She nodded before belatedly realizing she was standing there gaping at him like a ninny. And still holding on to his hand. She quickly released it. "I'm fine."

"Sorry about Arf. He never meant to hurt you. He's too puny to hurt a fly."

How nice. The guy had just likened her to a fly.

Clearly, Tom wasn't as impressed with her as she was with him. She must have imagined the flash of awareness in those awesome eyes of his.

"Arf goes out for his morning run every day. I hope you don't have a problem with that?"

Callie shook her head. But she had a feeling that she *would* have a problem fighting her emotions for a wounded warrior who clearly didn't want her anywhere near him.

Chapter Two

Tom decided it had been much too long since he'd held a woman in his arms. That had to be the reason for his reaction to Callie. The only acceptable explanation.

Okay, yeah, that strange sense of recognition had resurfaced. Maybe he'd met her before?

No, he'd have remembered her. That much he was sure of.

That and the fact that she was trouble he couldn't afford right now.

"What are you doing out here?" Tom demanded, his aggravation level increasing.

"Why? Do you have a problem with me being outside?" Callie countered. Her look warned him that he'd better not reply in the affirmative.

"I meant what were you actually doing? It looked like you were shadowboxing in slow motion or something."

"Haven't you heard of tai chi?"

"Isn't it some kind of drink?"

"That's chai tea. Tai chi is a form of Chinese meditation and exercise. It stimulates your natural energy."

Tom was feeling plenty stimulated. And he'd gotten that way simply by watching her in her black shorts and blue tank top. The material was stretched tight across the generous curve of her breasts in a way that indicated she was not wearing a bra. She had the creamy skin of a natural redhead. Her hair was piled on top of her head with casual disregard.

But there was no disregarding the way she made him feel. He'd seen more than his fair share of beautiful women in his lifetime but never one who'd affected him this way.

"Classical tai chi is based on the philosophy of yin and yang," she said in a teacher's voice, "which asserts that every entity needs to interact with a counterpart of its opposite nature in order to achieve balance."

Tom wondered if that was the old "opposites attract" thing. If so, he could relate. He was a man. She was a woman. Opposites attracting.

Trouble. She's trouble, he reminded himself.

"The junction between yin and yang is in the torso. The teacher I had explained that we've lost touch with our torsos. We only think of the dexterity of hands and feet but not the torso." Callie moved her hands from her shoulders to her hips to illustrate her point.

He was already much too fascinated with her torso.

"My teacher described the torso as the dull part of the body."

You'd have to be dead to think that Callie's torso was dull.

"Studies have shown that tai chi reduces blood pressure."

Not his.

"It helps reduce stress and achieve balance."

She was looking at him strangely. He had to say something. "Maybe you could teach it to Arf then. He could use some balance. He only has two speeds: off and on. The only time he's off is when he's asleep. Like I said before, then nothing wakes him up. But once he's awake, then he's…"

Tom's voice trailed off as he realized that he was babbling. About his dog, no less. How pitiful was that? Had he gotten so out of practice talking to a woman that he'd completely forgotten how to do it?

Of course, he hadn't misidentified most women as an exotic dancer the night before.

Tom cleared his throat. "Anyway, I'm sorry about Arf knocking you over."

"He just startled me, that's all. No harm done."

"Right." His tongue felt as unwieldy as his clumsy dog. "Feels like it's going to be another scorcher today."

Callie nodded, her ponytail swinging and bobbing against her right cheek. "Yeah. Well, I better get going or I'll be late for work."

"Right." Now he was repeating himself. Brilliant.

Tom stood there and watched Callie head back to her cabin.

"Nice move," Tom told Arf, who gave him a doggy grin with his tongue hanging out. "Don't you know that it's not polite to paw a woman without her permission?"

Arf just panted.

"Do not do it again. Understood?"

Arf responded by lifting his leg and relieving himself, narrowly missing Tom's bare feet.

Swearing under his breath, it occurred to him that some days it just didn't pay to get out of bed.

* * *

"You did what?" The question came from Paula Gui-terrez, a fellow teacher who was gulping coffee along with Callie in the staff room before the students arrived and classes began. They were the first ones in and had the place to themselves, not that that would last long.

Paula had taught at McBain Elementary School even longer than Callie had. With her short, dark hair, round face and ready grin, she was a favorite with both staff and students. Callie had bonded with her from the very beginning.

"I made an idiot of myself this morning," Callie rue-fully acknowledged.

"How did you do that exactly?"

"By blurting out a bunch of totally irrelevant facts about tai chi to Tom." Callie had already explained who Tom was earlier.

"What did he say?"

"Nothing. He just stood there half-naked looking sexy."

"Which half was naked?"

"The top half. I already told you that."

"I'm just trying to get a good visual."

"It was a *very* good visual," Callie couldn't resist noting. Closing her eyes, she could still picture him standing there wearing a look of surprise and a pair of navy-blue boxer shorts and nothing else.

"He really thought you were an exotic dancer?"

Callie's eyes flew open at Paula's words. "Remember, you swore not to tell a soul about that."

"I won't. Although it would have made a nice note in the monthly staff newsletter."

Callie waved a packet of sugar at Paula threateningly before pouring it into her red coffee mug, a gift from last year's class. Number One Teacher was written on it, but what made it unique were the drawings done in permanent marker by several of the children.

"So he's cute, huh?"

Callie shook her head. "Cute sounds too tame. He's very good-looking, but he's not very friendly."

"He has a dog. He can't be too bad."

"He's not happy having me for a neighbor."

"Why not?"

"I don't think it's anything against me personally—"

"I should hope not!" Paula sounded indignant at the very idea.

"I think he just likes his privacy," Callie continued.

"How long until your town house is finished?"

"Not until August. That's the latest estimate anyway."

"You know that if I had any spare room, you could have moved in with me."

Paula and her husband and two kids were already squished into a tiny two-bedroom ranch house.

"I know." Callie gave her a quick hug of thanks. "Don't worry about me. Things will work out fine."

"Between you and this Marine?"

Callie shook her head at the speculative look in her friend's dark-brown eyes. "Trust me, I have no intention of getting involved with a rich guy. And this guy is plenty rich. He's inherited part of the King Oil fortune."

"And what's wrong with rich guys?"

"They think they rule the world. Not a very good attitude."

"How do you know that?"

"I attended a ritzy private high school on a scholarship. There were plenty of rich kids there who took great pleasure in making my life miserable by taunting and bullying me." There were times when Callie could still hear their damaging insults in her head.

She quickly slammed the door on those disturbing memories.

"Rich kids aren't the only ones who are bullies," Paula pointed out.

"I realize that."

"Did this guy, Tom, seem like a bully to you?" Paula asked.

"No. But it would still be stupid to get involved with him."

"Is this the brother who was injured in the Middle East? In an ambush or something, wasn't it?"

Callie nodded.

"How many brothers are there?"

"Five. Tom is the youngest."

"You already seem to be an expert on the family."

"That's my grandmother's fault."

"What does she do, quiz you on the Kozlowskis?"

Callie laughed. "Just about. She's definitely taken Striker under her wing. He's her boss."

"Does your grandmother know about Tom mistaking you for an exotic dancer?"

"Are you kidding? No way I'd tell her that. She'd be madder than a rained-on rooster, to use one of her favorite phrases. Besides, Tom apologized."

"Before siccing his dog on you."

"He didn't do that. He's just the cutest little thing."

"The Marine?"

"His dog." Although Callie had to privately admit that the Marine wasn't hard to take, either. "Time to get to work."

"On the Marine?"

"No, on something even more challenging," Callie countered with a grin. "Twenty exuberant kindergartners."

"Insulted any women lately?" Striker asked Tom over his cellphone a few hours later.

"Why?" Tom retorted. "What have you heard?" Had Callie told her grandmother what had happened that morning? That Arf had attacked her...sort of.

"Nothing. I've heard nothing, but you sure sound guilty."

"And you sound crazy. What do you want?"

"To bug you. But I also need your assistance in a certain matter."

"What kind of matter?" Tom demanded suspiciously.

"It's not a big deal."

"Fine, then get someone else to do it."

"You don't even know what I'm going to ask you to do yet."

"I can already tell I don't want to do it."

"Since when do we only do what we want to do in this life?"

Tom wanted to say *since I almost got my leg blown off.* But that smacked too much of a weakness he wasn't about to admit he had even to himself, let alone to his oldest brother.

"Fine," Tom growled. "What do you want me to do?"

"Pick up a friend of mine whose car is in for repairs."

Striker sounded a little too casual, which triggered Tom's internal alarm. "What friend?"

"Does it matter?"

"If I'm supposed to pick up your friend someplace, you're going to have to tell me who it is sooner or later."

"Agree to do it first," Striker countered.

"Why should I?"

"Because I asked you to."

"You asked me to jump off the garage roof once and I didn't do that, either."

"That was a dare. Different thing entirely."

"Similar dumb idea."

"In your opinion."

"Which is the only one that matters at the moment."

"It's a simple-enough request."

"So was jumping off the roof."

"Just pick up someone from work and drive this friend a few miles to the garage."

"Does this someone have a name?"

"Yes."

"Are you going to tell me what it is?"

"It's Callie, my executive assistant's granddaughter. The kindergarten teacher."

"Who's not a stripper."

"Lucky for you, Tex hasn't heard about your faux pas."

"Faux pas?" Tom mocked. "You're sounding less like a Marine every day."

"Watch it," Striker growled.

"You can dish it out, but you can't take it, huh?"

"I can take anything you toss my way, baby brother."

"Except for Tex."

Striker cleared his throat.

Tom grinned. "Gotcha."

"Don't do anything to upset her," Striker warned. "Or Callie."

"In that case, maybe it would be safer to get someone else to do this favor for you."

"No one else is available or I would have called someone else."

Tom didn't know whether he should be pleased or insulted that he was on the bottom of Striker's wanted list for this assignment. "Fine. Give me the details."

Striker rattled off an address. "The SUV you're driving has a navigation system, so just punch in the address and it will tell you where to go."

Tom hated being told where to go. A recent development.

"And don't be late," Striker added.

"Don't worry, I'll protect you from the big bad Tex." Tom had to laugh at his brother's succinctly insulting reply before disconnecting.

A second later, his cellphone rang again. Assuming it was Striker, Tom said, "Having second thoughts already?"

"Second thoughts?" his mom repeated. "About what?"

"Nothing. I thought you were someone else."

"Anyone I know?"

"Your firstborn son."

"Ah, Striker. How have you two been getting along?"

Tom and Striker had always been somewhat at odds with each other. Maybe it was the fact that Striker was the oldest and Tom the youngest, born a minute after his twin brother, Steve. Maybe it was the fact that they were both equally stubborn and intense. Or maybe it was that garage-roof incident.

"Everything's fine," Tom replied.

"We plan on coming down to the ranch in time for the birth of Striker and Kate's new baby in a few weeks. We'll travel in the RV, of course."

"Of course." His parents loved that RV of theirs.

"Do you want to talk to your dad?"

"Sure."

Stan Kozlowski was a lot like his sons. A lifelong Marine, stubborn, proud, honorable and courageous.

"How's it going?" his dad said in that gruff, booming voice of his. Tom could instantly picture him—solidly built, his hair still buzz-cut short but going gray now. He continued to have a commanding presence that radiated authority.

"Good," Tom replied. "It's going good."

"Glad to hear it. Here's your mother."

His dad had never been one to gab on the phone.

"We may take a different route down this time and stop in Arkansas. We've never driven through that state."

"You guys still planning on hitting all fifty states with that RV?"

"That's the plan. But you can always reach us on the cellphone if you need anything."

"I know that."

"Hey, I'm your mom. It's my job to worry about you and all my kids."

"We're not kids anymore."

"I know that." His mom sighed. "You're all married and having kids of your own."

"Not me."

"No, not you. Not yet."

"Not anytime soon," Tom stated emphatically.

"Why not?"

"Plenty of reasons. Don't be in such a hurry to get me married off."

"I'm not. I just want you to be happy."

Tom didn't know how to answer that. Because the one thing that would make him happy was the one thing he couldn't have. His old life back.

Tom watched the American flag blowing in the wind as he sat in the SUV in front of McBain Elementary

School. He was early. The kids were still in class and so was Callie.

His gaze returned to the flag. He experienced a swell of pride every time he saw that star-spangled banner. As a Marine, he was willing to fight to the death for his country—for that flag and all it represented.

The ringing of the school bell sounded a moment before the doors burst open and kids poured out. The sea of rugrats made Tom wonder what it would be like to have a kid of his own. Sure, he had a niece and a nephew, and that was great. But what about being a dad?

A knock on the window startled him. Usually, he was aware of his surroundings, a result of his training. He was getting soft. Thinking about having kids? What was that all about?

The woman knocked again. He reluctantly lowered the window.

She smiled at him. "Hi there. Are you waiting for someone?"

"Yes, ma'am." Why else would he be here?

"Are you one of the parents? I don't recognize you, I'm sorry."

"No need to apologize, ma'am. And no, I'm not a parent."

"No?" Now she started eyeing him suspiciously, clutching her cellphone in one hand. "Who are you waiting for?"

"Callie. She teaches here."

The woman's face relaxed and her smile returned. Even bigger than before. "Hey, are you Tom Kozlowski? Captain Tom Kozlowski?"

He blinked in surprise.

"You are, aren't you? I'm so glad to meet you. My brother-in-law is a Marine."

While it was true that Marines were a close-knit bunch, contrary to popular belief, they did not all know one another.

"Hey, Rosie, come over here! This is Captain Kozlowski. We've heard all about you," the as-yet-unnamed woman cheerfully informed Tom.

"From whom?"

"Tex."

"Tex?" Was Striker's executive assistant a one-woman media outlet or what?

The first woman nodded excitedly. "I'm sorry, I didn't introduce myself. I'm Sandi. Part of the neighborhood watch group here. Hey, Donna, come over here." She waved down another mom who'd come to pick up her kids. "This is Captain Kozlowski. The one Tex told us about. The war hero."

Tom winced. No way did he want to carry that mantle. There were plenty of guys much more deserving than he was.

"I thought Captain Kozlowski ran King Oil?" one of the women said.

"That's Striker Kozlowski," another replied. "This is his brother Tom. The one injured in the Middle East."

What was it with women that they thought they could talk about you as if you weren't there?

He was really tempted to turn the key in the ignition and head on out of there.

"Come on, ladies, give the guy a break." The request came from Callie. She was wearing a denim skirt and a light-blue T-shirt. Nothing outstandingly fancy or sexy, so there was no reason for his body to react the way it did. Her hair was still piled on top of her head, a little neater than it had been this morning but still possessing a slightly ruffled look that made him imagine her surrounded by black satin sheets after a session of lovemaking that lasted most of the night. "You'll have him thinking you've never seen a good-looking Marine before."

The other women giggled before disbanding.

So Callie thought he was good-looking, did she? Nice to hear, given his current battered condition.

"You have funny eyebrows," the little girl next to Callie informed Tom.

Great. Another unwelcome and unwanted female opinion.

The kid ran off before he could think of a suitable answer. Just as well.

But a second later, another tiny female rugrat showed up to replace the first one. This one stood at Callie's side as if to defend her from him. The kid pointed at him. "You have a mark on your face. Did your sister scratch you?"

"I don't have a sister."

"You're lucky. Did your cat scratch you?"

"I don't have a cat."

"Were you in a fight?"

"Yes." He rubbed the fading scar with his thumb.

"We're not allowed to fight at school," she informed him. "And I'm not allowed to talk to strangers."

"Anna, this is Captain Kozlowski," Callie said.

"I don't know you," she told Tom.

"I don't know you, either," he said, getting aggravated by the kid's intense stare.

She stuck her tongue out at him and ran over to where her mom was waiting.

"Sorry about that," Callie said before adding, "What are you doing here?"

It was déjà vu all over again, to quote Yogi Berra. "Isn't this how we started out this morning?"

"No, then *you* were asking *me* what I was doing. Now I'm asking you."

"And we're both wearing more clothes."

She blushed. Tom hadn't seen a woman blush in years. It looked good on her.

"I'm here to take you to get your car," he said. "Striker sent me."

"I'm sorry. I mean, I'm sorry that he bothered you."

"He's my older brother. He lives to bother me. It's what he does best."

"And what do *you* do best?"

"I don't know anymore. I used to be a damn good Marine."

"And?"

"And what?"

"And what else were you good at?"

Her words surprised him.

So did her attitude.

She wasn't avoiding his gaze or staring at him with pity. Instead, she was almost issuing him a challenge.

"Football," he replied. "I was good at football."

"And?"

"And shooting pool."

"And?"

"Playing the accordion."

She blinked. "Really?"

He felt like an idiot for revealing that top secret bit of intel. "And kissing."

"Naturally. That's a given. All Marines who are good at football and the accordion are good at kissing."

Now she was mocking him. To his surprise, he liked it.

"I'm almost ready to go, but I have to clear up a few things first," she said. "Do you want to come in?"

Tom hesitated.

"Or you can wait out here and chat with the women…"

"I suppose I could come in for a minute."

His exit from the SUV was more awkward than he'd have liked and left him momentarily leaning on the hood as he repositioned his knee.

He wasn't hurting as badly as he had yesterday.

Some days were just better than others.

He hated having to use the cane at all, and he *really* hated doing so in front of so many people. But leaning on it was better than falling on his face.

To her credit, Callie didn't make a fuss over him, hover or make him feel like an invalid.

Sure, she may have slowed her walk a little to stay beside him. But she didn't object when he held the door open for her. In fact, she flashed him a smile, one of those surprisingly high-powered grenade-launching smiles that had shaken him to his core the first time he'd seen it.

"My classroom is right here."

Tom had been on enough recon missions to be able to size up a place in seconds. No hostile enemy forces here. He felt like a giant in this room designed for little rugrats. The plastic tables and chairs were tiny. One wall was mostly windows. The remaining walls were filled with bulletin boards, brightly colored artwork and displays. Beneath them were cubicles filled with books and toys.

"Must be a great job teaching kindergarten," he noted. "I mean, it's not like you give out homework or anything like that. You just let them play and stuff."

Tom could immediately tell by the look on her face that he'd said the wrong thing. "What?"

"I *teach*. I don't just sit here and watch the kids play."

"I didn't mean to imply that you were lazy or anything."

"Well, gee, thanks."

He shrugged. "I just meant, how hard can it be?"

Callie rolled her eyes. "Oh, that sounds much better. If I didn't think you were deliberately pushing my buttons, you'd be in deep trouble. Knee-deep in cow manure, in fact. Up to your armpits in alligators."

He had to grin. She was right. He *had* been pushing her buttons with that last comment of his. "So you're sensitive about your job, huh?"

"I love it and I take it seriously. Studies indicate that a child's capacity to learn is largely formed by the age of six. My class curriculum includes six main areas of learning." She ticked them off on her fingers. "Language arts, mathematics, science, music, art and social studies. And what you might consider 'just play' actually teaches communication and problem-solving skills. Early exposure to books and speech can mean that a child will have a 20,000-word vocabulary by the age of five rather than 5,000 words, which is the average for a child who is not often engaged in language."

"Okay, okay, enough already." He held up one hand to indicate his surrender. "I'm suitably impressed."

"I should hope so." Her stomach grumbled and she laughed self-consciously. "Sorry about that, but I had to skip lunch today for a meeting. Listen, after we get my car, would you like to stop somewhere for something to eat? My treat. It's the least I can do to thank you for helping me out this way."

She could see by the flash of surprise in his awesome eyes that her invitation had startled him.

His arrival here at school had totally startled her. He

had more clothes on than the last time she'd seen him. He looked respectable and formidable in a pair of jeans softened by numerous washings to fit his body to perfection and a simple dark-blue T-shirt with the initials U.S.M.C. on the front.

She was prepared for Tom to argue with her invitation, to get all prickly about a woman picking up the tab or to tell her he simply wasn't interested.

Instead, he surprised her yet again.

"Sure," he drawled. "Why not?"

Chapter Three

"Really?" Callie wanted to make sure she'd heard him correctly.

"You have a problem with me accepting your invitation?" Tom countered.

"No, it's just that I thought I'd have to convince you."

"And how did you plan on doing that?"

"I hadn't actually gotten that far. I suppose I would have done something like point out that we both have to eat so we might as well have dinner together. But that doesn't sound very convincing, does it? Let's see…maybe I would've used my charm? Smiled sweetly? Fluttered some eyelashes?" Callie illustrated her suggestion in such an exaggerated manner that he had to laugh. She grinned. "I know, I know. It's not really my style. I tend to be too direct to pull off the simpering sweetie thing very well."

Her eyes met his. Just like last night, she was once again struck by their color: an intriguing mixture of green and light brown.

Or was it the intensity she saw there that got to her?

Even now, with a glint of humor reflected in his gaze, there was a powerful intensity there.

This was a man who felt things deeply but was intent on hiding that fact.

Why? What had happened to this wounded warrior to make him erect barriers so high and so strong?

Callie didn't realize she'd reached out until her hand brushed his. The sensitized tips of her fingers registered the contact as an eight on the Richter scale.

Instant awareness.

Instant response.

"Oh, thank heavens you're still here." Paula rushed into the room with a little boy in hand.

Callie immediately moved away from Tom, feeling as guilty as one of her students caught eating candy in the middle of class.

"Can you look after Quentin until his mom gets here?" Paula asked. "He missed the bus again. She's downtown, so it will take her about twenty minutes to get here. I can't wait because my oldest daughter has a dentist appointment in fifteen minutes."

Callie shot a quick look at Tom, who nodded briefly. "No problem," Callie told Paula. "You go on ahead. We'll stay with him. Hi, Quentin." She flashed him a big smile.

Quentin just shuffled his feet and fingered his backpack.

"Come on in and make yourself comfortable. You can pull out something to play with if you like. Maybe some LEGO blocks?" Callie showed him where they were stored.

A few minutes later, Quentin had the colorful pieces spread out on a worktable and was engrossed in constructing something, his small fingers working with surprising speed. He paused occasionally to shove his glasses back up to the bridge of his nose, then resumed his intense concentration.

"Was he one of your kids last year?" Tom asked her.

Callie shot him a startled look. There was something about the way he said *your kids*, as if she had children of her own.

"No, Quentin moved here a few months ago." Seeing that the child was happy playing, she moved closer to her desk. "If you don't mind, I'll just finish up some work. I have some love letters…." Her voice trailed off at his raised eyebrow.

"Love letters?" Tom drawled. "Doesn't sound like work to me."

"They're written by my students."

"A little young for you, no?"

Callie perched on the corner of her desk, close enough to him to shoot him a reprimanding look but far enough away to avoid any unnecessary contact. "I have a canvas bag wrapped around the back of the chair at my desk. The kids slip notes in it during the day."

"Complaining about the food? Asking for shorter nap times?"

"Expressing their feelings."

Tom wrinkled his forehead as if she'd said a foul word.

"Marines don't have feelings?" she challenged.

"They get in the way."

"They do? Of all the nerve. How impolite of them."

His startled gaze met hers. She could tell that he wasn't accustomed to someone mocking him.

She could also tell that she was fascinated by his eyes. She felt as if she could drown in them. Silly but true.

She leaned closer.

So did he.

The sound of a plastic LEGO block hitting the table brought her to her senses. She scooted off the desk, headed around to the mailbag and gathered up the notes to read later that evening.

"What are you making?" Tom addressed the question to Quentin.

The child just shrugged and didn't look up.

Tom moved closer. "Looks impressive."

"It's a megablaster."

"What does it do?"

"It's like a gun, only better. We're not allowed to play with guns at school."

Tom nodded in agreement with that policy, his attention focused on sitting in one of the few grown-up chairs in the room without making an idiot of himself. Mission accomplished.

"I like to play army because then you can get the bad guys," Quentin said.

"Playing Marines is even better," Tom immediately replied. "Talk about bad guys. Marines can beat them hands down."

Quentin frowned. "Why would they put their hands down? Is it because putting your hands up means you're a scaredy-pants weenie?"

"*Hands down* is just a phrase. It means 'easily.' Marines always beat the bad guys. It's their job."

"Mine, too. My army...I mean, my Marines get the bad guys. Then they can't get me."

"Do you have bad guys after you?"

Quentin nodded solemnly. "Yeah. But if I had a megablaster for real, they wouldn't mess with me. Are you a Marine? I heard them talking about it outside."

"Yeah, I'm a Marine."

"Can I hire you to get the bad guys or do you do that as part of your job?"

"Depends on what bad guys you're talking about."

"What if there were bad guys here at school?"

"Then you should talk to a teacher about that."

"Then I'd be a tattletale scaredy-pants weenie."

Callie joined in on the conversation for the first time. She'd overheard it all with a heavy heart. Quentin had moved into their school district halfway through the school year—always a traumatic thing for a child. "It's not tattling. If someone makes you feel unsafe and you ask them to stop and they don't, then it's not tattling to tell an adult. It's the correct thing to do. Because no one has the right to make you feel unsafe."

Quentin looked to Tom as if for confirmation. Tom nodded in agreement before adding, "We describe that in the Marine Corps as calling in reinforcements. And reporting to our chain of command."

Quentin's brown eyes widened behind the lenses of his glasses. "You mean you have teachers in the Marines?"

Tom nodded again. "I had to take lots of classes to become a Marine."

"And read books?"

"Yes, and read books."

"Sounds hard."

"It is, but it's worth it."

"Did you get that scar by getting beat up by the bad guys?"

Tom nodded. "They didn't fight fair."

"Bad guys don't most of the time, do they?"

Truer words were never spoken. "No."

"So how do you win if they don't fight fair?"

"By calling in reinforcements."

"Does that work?"

"Yes."

"As good as a megablaster?"

"Even better."

"That's hard to believe."

"I know."

They were interrupted by the arrival of Quentin's mom. Callie took her aside to speak to her privately in the hallway while Quentin continued playing and talking to Tom.

"Hi, we haven't met before. My name is Callie Murphy and I'm a kindergarten teacher here. Mrs. Guiterrez asked me to look after Quentin until you got here, as she had a dentist appointment. I was just wondering. Has Quentin been missing the bus a lot lately?"

The woman shot her a frazzled look. "Yes. I've talked to him about it and he promised me he'd do better."

"Has he said *why* he misses the bus?" Callie prompted.

"I'm not sure. He might not like some of the kids on it."

"I think he's being bullied," Callie said.

"He never told me that."

"He may have been afraid to say anything."

"Why? I certainly wouldn't yell at him for telling me he was being bullied."

"I'm sure you wouldn't. But Quentin may have been afraid of repercussions if he told anyone what was really happening."

"How do you know he's being bullied? Did you see it happening?"

"No."

"Then maybe he's just exaggerating. You know how boys can be."

"Yes, I do. And I know how bullies can be. And what damage they can do."

"My husband tells me that Quentin has to learn to defend himself instead of being such a..." His mom waved her hand as if unwilling to say the actual word, whatever insulting word it might have been.

Callie held her temper in check. She'd dealt with parents like this before, but it still never failed to amaze her how unenlightened some of them could be. "This school has a zero-tolerance policy for bullying."

"That seems a little extreme."

"Not when you consider the long-lasting damage that bullying can do. It's one of the leading social problems facing schools and young people today. Studies have shown that children and adolescents who bully are more likely to become violent adults, more likely to abuse their own children and more likely to commit serious crimes. Bullying is a form of abuse, and the victims can end up with a lifetime of low self-esteem, depression, anxiety problems and fear of social relationships."

The other woman's eyes widened. "I had no idea."

"That information, along with the school's policy, was in the parent packet that you received when you registered Quentin."

"I haven't really had time to look it over," Quentin's mom admitted.

"There was a form you had to return to the school stating that you'd read the material."

"I just signed it and returned it with him to class. I just never thought of bullying as a type of abuse. I mean, as a parent, I certainly wouldn't stand by and watch my child being physically abused by someone else. I won't stand by and let this happen, either."

"Good. Mrs. Guiterrez will be in touch with you regarding the actions that will be taken to improve the situation for Quentin."

"What can I do to help?"

"Talk to Quentin. Ask him what's going on at school and have him tell you about his day. Really listen to him and respect what he has to say. Try to focus just on him and not anything else while he's speaking to you."

"I'm usually making dinner when he tells me about school. I don't really hear most of what he says."

"Set some time aside to listen to Quentin. I understand that it's hard to find time for everything, but this is important."

"I see that now. Thanks for talking to me."

Once Quentin had left with his mom, Tom spoke out. "What kind of parents name their kid Quentin? They might as well have painted a big target on the kid's back. What were they thinking?"

"There's no excuse."

"You said it."

"I meant there's no excuse for bullying," Callie fiercely stated.

He eyed her thoughtfully. "You seem pretty passionate about it."

"Absolutely. I've seen the damage it can do."

"I can't picture anyone bullying you."

If only he knew.

"I think I've died and gone to Heaven." Tom just about moaned in pleasure.

"You like?" Callie's voice was breathless.

"Oh yeah."

"Do you want more?"

"Mmm."

"Here you go." She placed another stack of barbe-cued baby back ribs on his plate. "Now aren't you glad I brought you here?"

Here was Jimmy Bob's Barbecue, where the decor was down-home simple. Red-and-white-checked oil-cloth covered the tables, while Texas memorabilia covered the walls. But the customers didn't come here for the ambience. They came to indulge in the eating experience, getting spicy sauce all over their fingers and sometimes even on their faces.

This wasn't the place for a romantic tryst, which was one of the reasons Callie had chosen it. That and the incredible food.

"Good, huh?" she said again, since Tom hadn't responded to her last question and had instead immediately begun to dig into the next helping of ribs.

Barbecue sauce looked mighty good on that stubborn chin of his.

"Texans take their barbecue very seriously, you know," she told him.

"They take everything seriously."

"Learning that, are you?"

Tom wiped the sauce from his chin, then licked his fingers, drawing her attention to their lean length.

"This entire thing has been a learning experience," he said.

"And what have you learned so far?"

"That I don't like being treated like one of the walking wounded all the time. I don't want you seeing me that way," he warned her.

"I don't," she instantly assured him. "I see you as

stubborn and crabby but surprisingly compassionate when you want to be. You were really great with Quentin today."

"What did you think I was going to do to the kid?"

"I don't know. Put on your big bad Marine act with him."

"It's no act."

She blew a raspberry at him.

He put on his war face.

"Very impressive." Callie nodded approvingly. "But there's no going back now. I know you have a heart someplace under that gruff exterior."

He scowled. "Don't go getting all sappy just because I was nice for a moment or two."

"Oh, don't worry. I'm not the sappy sort."

"I'm glad to hear it, but I have to warn you that it can be dangerous to blow raspberries at a crabby Marine. Especially when you're eating barbecue."

"Stop complaining." She grinned and stuck her tongue out at him. "I didn't get any barbecue sauce on you. I made sure of that." She paused to take another bite and then wiped her cheek. The spicy sauce was delicious, but it did get all over. "I told you this was the best barbecue in Texas."

"What is it with Texans that they have to have the best of everything?"

"You don't consider yourself a Texan?"

"I consider myself a Marine."

"You didn't grow up around here?"

"I grew up all over. We moved around a lot, as my dad got various postings."

"I've always lived in this area."

"I got that impression. From your accent."

"I don't have an accent. *You* do."

"How do you figure that?"

"Paloma, do I have an accent?" she called out to the hostess who'd shown them to their table earlier. A frequent customer, Callie knew just about everyone who worked here.

"No. No accent."

Callie turned back to Tom. "See?"

He saw, all right. Saw her. Smiling at him. With sauce on her face.

She thought she'd gotten it all when she wiped her cheek, but she hadn't.

She looked so darned cute.

No, that wasn't right. *Cute* described puppies. And cute had never made his mouth water.

Tom was fascinated by her. She was a breath of fresh air in his life.

His attention focused on her lips. The moment he met her, he'd noticed her red hair and her sinful lips.

And when they'd almost kissed, something monumental had happened.

Why was that?

He didn't like not knowing these things. He preferred to have the upper hand in any kind of male-female situation. Not that he was dominating. But he wasn't one to give in to emotions.

Except for that one slipup with Penny. But she'd caught him at a vulnerable moment, shortly after his injuries.

He refused to ever be that vulnerable again.

But that didn't mean he couldn't enjoy watching Callie's expression of bliss as she licked her lips.

"What?" She blinked, suddenly noticing his attention. "Do I have something on my face?"

"Yeah, a smile."

"Something wrong with that?"

"I guess not. I haven't been exposed to many smiles lately."

"Because you're so crabby."

"I meant to comment on that mistaken observation earlier."

"Go right ahead. Give it your best shot." She'd grown accustomed to arguing with him before making him see reason. Was even looking forward to it. "Try and convince me you're not crabby."

"I've been known to be charming on occasion."

"Really? I can't imagine that," she teased him. "What kind of occasions? Weddings and baptisms? That sort of thing?"

"On dates. With women."

"I already figured you knew how to be charming with women. Not that I could tell that right off the bat."

"I already explained about that."

"Not very well."

"You're just full of compliments for me tonight, aren't you?"

"I didn't think you really needed to hear more compliments. I've got a feeling that you've collected more than your fair share of them over the years."

"Oh yeah?"

"Yeah. Am I right?"

He wasn't sure how to answer that one. "That's one of those tricky questions women ask."

"Really? Funny, it seemed pretty straightforward to me."

"Seems to me I hang myself no matter what I say, so let's change the subject."

"Sure. You pick one you like."

"Have you always wanted to be a teacher?"

"Pretty much. Have you always wanted to be a Marine?"

"Originally I wanted to be a Jedi Knight from *Star Wars.*"

"Really? Me, too. Wow, finally something we have in common."

"You didn't want to be the princess?"

"No way. Too hard to run in that dress."

He had to laugh. Just when he thought he had her pegged, she threw him for a loop. "So how did you go from a fighter to a teacher?"

"Better job opportunities."

"Yeah, I felt that way about the Marines, too."

"I understand you come from a family of Marines."

"That's right. My dad was a Marine. An enlisted man. My brothers are all Marines. Or were. As you know, Striker is running the oil company now. My brothers Rad and Ben are stationed in North Carolina, and my brother Steve is at Camp Pendleton in California. He just got married recently. To a librarian. They got married in Las Vegas."

"That must have been fun."

"I wasn't there. I was recovering in Germany. But I was at my brother Rad's wedding." Tom had no idea why he was telling her all this. He'd never mentioned the words *wedding* and *marriage* so frequently in such a short period of time to any female in his entire life.

"Are all your brothers married?" Callie asked.

"Yeah, I'm the only remaining bachelor and I plan on keeping it that way."

"You don't have to say it as if you're warning me. I'm not looking to lasso you into matrimony or anything, so relax. There's nothing to be afraid of."

"Marines know how to overcome fear."

"So you admit you're afraid of marriage?"

"That's another one of those tricky questions."

"Ah, we women are a tricky lot, aren't we? Tossing all these questions at the poor man trying to eat his dinner in peace."

"You've got that right."

"Anyone ever told you that you're more than just a little old-fashioned?"

"I thought you Texans went for that."

"What? Men who think women should be seen and not heard? *Au contraire.* Texas women have a history of being independent and tough and strong."

"I'm impressed."

"You should be. Those women were impressive."

"I meant I was impressed with you."

"Me?"

"Yeah. You speak your mind."

Callie grinned. "I did warn you about that trait of mine."

"I like it."

"You do?"

"Yeah."

"That's not why I do it."

"I know. I like that, too."

His greenish brown eyes were expressive and intense.

Mesmerizing.

A silly word for the way he made her feel.

Well, he made her feel a lot of things actually. As if she were riding a merry-go-round at warp speed. As if he could see into the innermost recesses of her heart. As if he knew how to provide her with more pleasure than she'd ever experienced or even dreamed of experiencing in her entire life.

She grabbed her almost-empty glass of iced tea. "Uh, are you ready for dessert?"

"I can handle anything you dish up."

She could only imagine the sensual delights he could dish up.

Stop that, she ordered herself. Do *not* get sappy. "Lucky for you, I wasn't planning on making the dessert myself."

"You're not a good cook?"

"I can be sometimes. It's a bit of a gamble. Sometimes things turn out fine, sometimes they don't."

"Sounds like life."

"I guess it does." Callie paused a moment. What had they been talking about before? It took her a moment to remember. "So what about dessert? They have a wicked brownie concoction here. We could share if you want?"

Tom wanted to share all right. More than just a brownie. Why her? Why now? What was it about this woman in particular?

He'd always been one to follow policy by the book. But none of his Marine Corps training had prepared him for a sexy kindergarten teacher who didn't even try to get on his good side.

Sure, Callie was independent and had a feisty temper when provoked, but she also possessed a surprising vulnerability that made him want to gather her up in his arms.

True, the fact that she was beautiful and sexy might have something to do with him wanting her in his arms. But it wasn't the only reason.

"If you don't want to share, that's okay," she told him.

"Oh, I want to." His voice was rough with hunger.

Her eyes widened with recognition that he might be talking about more than just dessert here.

"Um, uh, okay then," she said, her words stumbling over one another.

The predator in him couldn't resist moving in. Leaning closer, he kept his eyes on hers. "So you want to?"

Her tongue darted out to lick her lips. Was she deliberately trying to drive him crazy? "Uh, I guess so."

"You're not sure?"

She narrowed her eyes and stared at him as if trying to read his thoughts. No way he'd let her.

Then her expression changed as she appeared to reach some kind of decision. Her earlier confidence returned, erasing her momentarily flustered state. "Listen, Captain, we're talking about a chocolate brownie here. The only reason I'm hesitating is that I might want it all for myself."

"That's the only reason your voice got all breathless, huh? It was the brownie?"

"Absolutely."

"Had nothing to do with me, is that right?"

"That's right."

Tom wasn't about to call Callie a liar to her face. But his expression indicated his doubts as to her veracity.

"For your information, I take chocolate very seriously," she informed him.

"I should be honored that you're willing to share with me then."

"You've got that right."

Tom thought that watching her eat barbecue was unexpectedly arousing, but that had nothing on watching her delicately consume the so-called wicked chocolate brownie.

She was incredibly sensual in her delight of every morsel. Tom was so distracted that he barely ate a bite.

Callie didn't seem to notice. Her attention was totally focused on the dessert. His was totally focused on her.

On her lips.

Her luscious mouth.

The rosy tip of her tongue darting up to lick her lips.

He shifted in his seat as his body reacted to the performance she was putting on.

He couldn't get that picture out of his head, even as he followed her home, watching the red taillights of her car in front of his.

He'd been so distracted that he was only now realizing that he'd allowed her to pay for his dinner. He never let a woman do that.

But then Callie was proving to be one of a kind.

Darkness had just fallen when they reached the cabins. A big moon was rising over the horizon, all orange and fat looking.

Tom made a point of being there to open her car door. She seemed surprised by his actions. Without saying a word, he offered her his hand.

As she had earlier that morning, she paused a second before taking it.

But unlike this morning, this time when Callie stood close to him, Tom gave in to his overwhelming urge to kiss her.

Chapter Four

Callie hadn't seen this coming. Not the kiss. Not the promise of ecstasy his mouth was imprinting on her very soul.

When Tom had pulled her into his arms, she'd dropped everything. Her oversize purse. Her car keys. Her defenses.

She was both startled and thrilled by his passionate invasion. Not that his approach was overly forceful. No smashing of lips or bumping of noses here.

Instead, he'd tipped her chin up and leaned down until his mouth completely covered hers, his lips warm and skilled as he taught her a new level of pleasure. The circling and tasting of his tongue was an erotic declaration of intent that she didn't want to deny.

She parted her lips, allowing him entry. He rewarded her, his tongue stroking hers convincingly.

The circle of his arms grew smaller as he molded her more tightly against him. She could feel the warmth of his body through the soft cotton of her T-shirt and his.

As their kiss deepened, Tom slid one hand down to her waist and beneath her T-shirt. She shivered with delight at the feel of his work-roughened fingertips on the bare skin at the small of her back.

He incorporated her moan into their kiss, the thrust of his tongue making her ache with unexpected desire. He continued his exploration of her bare skin with one hand while twining the other into her hair, loosening the fastener. He threaded his fingers through the silky strands, massaging her head.

She wanted more.

Callie tugged him closer just as the cellphone in her purse rang. Startled by the noise, she pulled back, which threw Tom off balance.

His cane clattered to the ground, even as he grabbed for the side of her car to stop himself from falling.

Only years of self-discipline kept Tom from swearing out loud. He'd almost fallen flat on his face. The moment of humiliating vulnerability hit home hard, reminding him how banged up he still was.

In the past, Tom had always been strong and powerful—the perfect Marine. Now he felt less like a man and not worthy of saddling a woman with his battered body and possible medical issues.

As an officer, he'd learned to lead by example. He ate last to make sure his Marines were fed. He had to be more proficient and better cross-trained than his men. The bottom line had always been that you can't lead if you can't do it yourself.

At the moment, he couldn't do much for himself. He couldn't even run half a mile. He could barely hobble around.

Several operations and a year in rehab had brought him back to maybe sixty percent of his fighting strength. On a good day. He had to battle back for more every day.

That's where his focus had to remain. Not on a sexy redhead who could have any man she wanted, not a guy whose best days might be behind him.

"Look, I'm not interested in starting anything right now," Tom bluntly told her.

He could tell he'd embarrassed her. "Me, either." She quickly dove down to gather up her belongings from the ground, including the cellphone she'd never answered. "Let's just forget that kiss happened, okay?"

He nodded.

Callie rushed away, and it was only once she was safely inside her cabin that she realized that she hadn't offered to help him get his cane.

She kept the lights off as she turned back the curtain to sneak a peek and make sure he was okay. She waited until he'd entered his cabin before letting the curtain fall back into place.

A quick glance at the caller ID on her cellphone told her that the call was from Paula.

Callie wasn't ready to speak to anyone yet. She needed to regain her composure first.

One thing was certain. Jimmy Bob's Barbecue might pack a punch, but it was nothing compared to Tom's fiery kiss.

Forgetting that fact would *not* be easy.

But he'd made it clear that he had no interest in continuing things between them. And he'd done that when she'd reached for him. Almost knocking him off his feet in her inexperienced eagerness.

She sank into the couch and held her hands to her

flushed cheeks. She felt like an idiot. Like an oversexed idiot.

One important lesson she'd learned: kissing Tom was as dangerous as smoking in a fireworks factory, as her gran would say.

Falling for him would be even more explosive. And more hazardous.

The next morning, Callie had her hands full at work when one of her most challenging students, Adam I-have-to-be-first-in-line, was even more of a handful than usual.

"Why are you acting up so much today, Adam?"

"My blood sugar is off," he informed her.

The first time Callie had heard that excuse she'd been a little freaked out and had checked with his mom, who told her that her husband used that as an excuse. Adam had picked up the phrase from him.

"No, it's not," Callie said. "Now put your toy away so we can do storytime."

Adam stomped off yelling, "I hate school! I'm never coming back!"

In the end, his behavior was so bad that Callie had to accompany him to principal Jeff Sanchez's office.

"What seems to be the problem, Adam?" Jeff asked.

Adam leaned forward in his chair to confide, "I'm really a secret agent. I have my orders."

There was a moment of stunned silence. Then Jeff asked, "Who's giving you your orders?"

"They come in a van."

Jeff didn't bat an eyelid while Callie had to bite the inside of her cheek to keep from laughing out loud. Of all her students, Adam had the most vivid imagination. You had to love him, even when you were nearing your wit's end.

"I see. Well, Adam, even secret agents have to follow the rules. Understand? Do you think you can go back to class and behave now?" Jeff asked in his no-nonsense voice.

Adam sat up straight, eager to leave. "Yes."

And so Callie took him back to class, smiling to herself all the way down the hallway.

No one could say her job was boring. She loved teaching and she loved her students. Loved watching them develop and bloom, gain confidence and skills. They never ceased to amaze her.

Especially Adam, who leaned against her leg as they returned to the classroom and looked up at her with those big eyes of his. "You're my favorite teacher in the entire universe!"

She smoothed his dark hair away from his forehead and smiled down at him even as her heart softened with affection. He was a little rascal, but he had his moments.

Dealing with twenty exuberant, overactive kindergartners was definitely not for wimps. The job required patience, imagination, discipline, and lots of love.

Her day's work wasn't done once the children left for the day. First, she had paint pots to clean up. Then she had to prepare for the next day's lessons.

Callie had just completed the day's record keeping when Paula stopped by. "I just wanted to give you an update on Quentin. Jeff set up a meeting with the children involved—two fifth graders—and their parents."

"I'm so glad Jeff is implementing the zero-tolerance bullying policy at this school. As the principal, he really does need to set the standards and make sure that they are adhered to."

"Hard to do in an environment where some Texans

think that kind of behavior is good for toughening up children."

"I know. But you know the facts as well as I do. Bullying is a form of abuse."

"Hey, you don't have to convince me."

Callie nodded. "I know, I'm preaching to the choir here."

"That program you started last year where sixth graders mentor kindergartners has really been a big success," Paula noted. "They're very protective of the little ones once they get to know them."

"My little guys drew pictures of their buddy-mentors and wrote stories about them. And the sixth graders interviewed the little ones to make a digital video about the class."

"It's going to be hard when the sixth graders move on to middle school."

"I've told my class that their buddy-mentors will come back to visit. And they can e-mail them. The reduction of bullying incidents among the sixth graders has been dramatic. But it has to start young. That's why we spend so much time right from the start on the classroom rules of respecting others and being kind."

"And you know firsthand the damage that can be done, having been bullied yourself," Paula said.

Callie nodded. The constant tormenting, the verbal cruelties and the ostracizing had left permanent scars on her psyche. They might not be the kind of scars you could see, but they were equally painful and ran deep into her soul.

She'd been a very late bloomer, not coming into her own until she was halfway through college when the ugly duckling she'd been had finally turned into a swan.

But by then the damage had been done. Callie never

forgot those earlier years of humiliation. She got past them, but she couldn't seem to really get over them.

"Money makes a lot of people arrogant," Callie said.

"Some of us are arrogant to begin with," Tom drawled from the doorway.

"I wasn't talking about you," Callie quickly assured him.

"Glad to hear it."

Seeing him brought back the memory of being in his arms the other night.

She'd tried to stuff the images into a mental box and thought she'd succeeded until this moment. Now they all popped up like a jack-in-the-box.

The feel of his mouth on hers.

The thrust of his tongue.

The roughness of his fingers brushing her bare skin.

Callie reached for a folder and started fanning herself before realizing what she was doing. She immediately stopped and tried to look confident and in control. No easy feat given the fact she just realized she had green finger paint on her arm. "What are you doing here?"

"I brought your love letters."

"What?" Her heart skipped for a second at the thought of him writing a declaration of his desire for her. Had he regretted pushing her away after kissing her? Had he changed his mind about not wanting to get involved with her?

"The notes your kids wrote. They must have fallen out of your bag in my SUV."

"Oh." Callie stood there a moment. Then she moved forward to take the papers he held in his hand, taking extreme care to ensure that her fingers didn't actually touch his.

Concentrating on that made Callie forget her manners, forcing her friend to introduce herself.

"Hi, I'm Paula Guiterrez." She held out her hand. "I saw you when I was rushing off to a dental appointment a few days back, but we weren't formally introduced."

"Pleased to meet you, ma'am. Captain Tom Kozlowski at your service."

"At my service, huh?" Paula teased him. "Be careful what you say, Captain, or we might put you to work around here."

"Call me Tom."

"And you can call me Paula."

"Didn't you have report cards you had to work on?" Callie asked her.

"What?"

Callie gave her a meaningful look.

Paula got the message. "Oh right. Report cards. A teacher's work is never done."

"I thought you got the summers off," Tom said.

Paula rolled her eyes.

"Don't get us started," Callie warned him. Once they were alone, she said, "Thanks for bringing these back, but you could have just left them on my front porch or something. You didn't have to drive all the way over here."

"It was on my way."

"Your way where?"

"Where I'm going." Tom had no intention of telling her that he'd made the trip just to see her. His mornings were spent in physical therapy. His afternoons were spent thinking about her and that kiss he'd vowed to forget.

"Oh. Well, thanks for dropping them off."

"You're welcome. By the way, I had a little talk with Quentin outside."

"You did?"

"Affirmative. And you can wipe that expression off your face."

"What expression?"

"That horrified what-have-you-done look."

Callie immediately tried for a calm smile. "Is this better?"

"A little."

"So what did you talk to Quentin about?"

"Bad guys. And how to deal with them."

"Oh no." She couldn't help it. The horrified expression had returned to her face and traveled to her voice, as well.

"Yeah," Tom drawled. "I told him that a hand grenade pretty well takes care of things."

"You didn't!"

"Of course I didn't," he growled. "Do you think I'm a complete idiot?"

"Well, no."

"Gee, thanks for the ringing endorsement."

"It's just that you're a Marine."

"Which means I like blowing things up, is that it?"

"No. But as a Marine, you do have a different mind-set."

"True, which is why I was able to help Quentin."

"You still haven't told me what you said to him."

"And after your reaction, I'm not inclined to."

Callie just gave him a look, one that even made the class troublemaker, Adam, sit up and take notice.

It had no effect on this big bad Marine.

Tom just folded his arms across that broad chest of his and stared right back at her.

"You're not using your cane," she belatedly noted.

"Don't change the subject."

"You're the one who didn't want to tell me what you said to Quentin."

"I don't want to talk about my injury, either."

"Is your leg improving?"

"Some. Not enough."

"Enough for what?"

"To return to active duty."

"And that bothers you."

"No. Ants at a picnic *bother* me," he growled. "This goes way beyond that."

"I understand."

"I doubt that."

"Then you'd be wrong. It wouldn't be the first time."

One dark brow lifted. "You're never going to let me forget that, are you?"

"You thinking I was an exotic dancer? No, I don't think I will. It's too much fun pushing your buttons about it."

"You know," he drawled, "a sweet little kindergarten teacher oughta be careful about pushing a tough Marine's buttons—or any other part of his anatomy. She might end up getting more than she bargained for."

That she could believe.

"You do that drawl mighty fine," she complimented him. "Almost the way a real Texan would."

"You don't appear to be taking my threat seriously."

"If it were a serious threat, I would."

"Oh, I was serious, darlin'."

Okay, he definitely had the *darlin'* down pat, better than she'd ever heard it said before by any Texan anywhere. And definitely more powerful in its effect on her.

Why was that?

She knew better than to go all hormonal over a wealthy man. Especially one who was only in town for a short period of time. Tex had told her that Tom was only staying with Striker until he'd recovered enough to return to the Marines.

But Tom had just said that he wasn't ready yet for active duty. What if he never was?

That still didn't mean he'd stay in Texas.

"You don't believe me?" he growled.

"I believe you. Uh, what was it you said again?" she teased.

He shook his head in disapproval. "You're not payin' attention. And in a classroom. Big mistake."

"If you were the teacher, yes. But you're not. *I'm* the teacher here."

"You don't think there's anything I could teach you?"

"Oh, I'm sure there's plenty you could teach me. I don't know how useful it would be, however."

"Who said anything about useful?"

"I just did."

"Useful isn't what makes the world go 'round."

"Sure it is. Well, actually there's a complicated scientific reason for the Earth's rotation—"

He interrupted her to say, "Do you ever stop talking?"

"Not very often."

Her eyes met his as she remembered that kiss the other night.

His kiss had stopped her from talking. And almost stopped her from breathing while flooding her entire body with a wave of passionate longing.

Was he thinking about that kiss, too? Is that why his eyes became all dark and even more…mesmerizing?

She searched for some kind of clue as to what his thoughts were, but he looked away as if determined not to share them with her.

"I better get going," he said gruffly.

He left quickly, but thoughts of him remained with Callie long afterward—along with the memory of how unexpectedly right it had felt to be held in his arms.

Chapter Five

"Hey, Tommy, how are those hallucinations going?"

His twin, Steve, was the only one who got away with calling him Tommy. "What are you babbling about?"

"Striker tells me you're hallucinating now, mistaking kindergarten teachers for strippers."

"Ha-ha. Very funny. You two should take your act on the road."

"What's wrong? Is our big brother getting on your nerves?"

"Maybe staying here wasn't such a good idea after all," Tom muttered, sinking into the couch and propping his good leg on the coffee table, where Arf jumped up to lick his bare toes.

"Why not? What's going on?"

"Nothing's going on. Why does something have to be going on?"

"Because you sound crabbier than a bear in heat."

"I thought Texas sayings were Striker's specialty."

"Doesn't mean I can't come up with a good one myself every now and then."

"If you ever do come up with a good one, you let me know." He heard Steve's burst of laughter over the phone line.

"So why are you calling me anyway?" Tom demanded. "I thought you'd be immersed in married life."

"Hey, you're the one who told me to get married, and sent me back here to the States when I came to your bedside in Germany."

"It was the meds talking."

"Now you tell me."

"So what's the problem?"

"Who says anything's wrong? Can't a guy just call his brother? His twin brother?"

"His smarter twin brother," Tom added.

"Says you."

"Says everyone. Even Busha knows you're not the sharpest knife in the drawer."

"Hey!" Steve immediately protested. "Our grandmother loves me dearly. I'm her favorite, you know."

"Dream on," Tom scoffed.

"She introduced me to my wife."

"She was matchmaking again. And you were dumb enough to fall for it."

"It was the smartest thing I ever did."

"Considering that you're not the sharpest knife—"

"I could always send Busha to hook you up with someone," Steve threatened. "I hear she's coming down in a few weeks to be there for Striker's baby's birth."

"Thanks for the warning."

"So what's with the teacher?"

"She knows I can play the accordion," Tom abruptly blurted out.

"You told her?" Steve sounded shocked. "No one knows except for you and me and Busha. You never tell anyone about that."

"It just came out."

"You realize what this means, don't you?" Steve said.

"Yeah," he muttered, "that she knows I can play a dorky instrument."

"It means she knows your secret."

"Not all of them." She didn't know about the fierce battle between hope and fear raging inside Tom. No one did. He planned on keeping it that way.

"Maybe not, but it's a start."

"The start of what?"

"Your downfall."

Tom rolled his eyes. "What is it with you married guys? The minute you get hitched, you try to drag the rest of us down with you."

"Hey, I've been married more than a minute."

"So I should be grateful that you waited this long to declare my downfall?"

Steve ignored his comment. "How did this top secret intel come out regarding the aforementioned musical instrument?"

"She asked me what I was good at," Tom muttered.

"And you said playing the accordion? You're slipping, man."

"I know. It's weird. When I'm with her, it's like I forget how to talk to a woman."

"Uh-oh."

"What? More proclamations of downfalls?"

"You'll see for yourself soon enough."

"I also told her I was good at football and shooting pool and kissing."

"What a lie! You stink at shooting pool."

"Says you, who can't even sink a two-foot straight-line shot in the pocket."

"Easy for you to challenge me, Tommy, when you're halfway across the country."

"Yes, I know."

Steve's voice turned serious. "And I hope that you know if you want to…you know, well, talk or anything…I'm here for you. Whatever, whenever."

"I know." Tom's voice was as gruff as his twin's. They'd always shared a special bond. He knew Steve was there for him 24/7.

"Hey, remember that time we tried mind reading as kids when we first played poker?" Steve asked.

Tom smiled. "Yes. It didn't work out."

"So that means you're gonna have to tell me if there's something wrong. I know you've had a tough time. And I know that your view of the female population may be a little tainted by that experience you had with that gold digger. What was her name again?"

"Penny."

"Listen, I went through a similar thing, remember? With Gina. I thought she was smart and classy and in love with me. Instead, she was in love with my bank account. One of the hazards of being a Marine with money."

"So I guess that proves we're both gullible when a pretty face comes along."

"Does this teacher of yours have a pretty face?"

"She's not *mine,* and yes. She has red hair and blue eyes, and even though she's sort of a petite little thing, she stands up to me and doesn't let me get away with anything."

Steve whistled. "I like her already."

"You've already got a wife."

"Also known as 'the best thing that ever happened to me.'"

Tom had gotten to meet Steve's wife, Chloe, when he'd first been shipped from the hospital in Germany to a military hospital in the States. She looked like a librarian, with her glasses and nice clothing. She had a great smile, though. He remembered that. And kind eyes.

"Did I mention that her grandmother works for Striker?" Tom said. "As his executive assistant."

"This female is Tex's granddaughter? Oh man, you are playing with fire, little brother."

"Cut the *little* stuff. I'm only one minute younger than you are and two inches taller."

"Says the fun-loving one in the family."

"Not lately," Tom noted quietly.

"Well, maybe this teacher will teach you how to have fun again. I taught Chloe how to have fun and ended up married to her."

"Marriage is not my idea of fun."

"How little you know."

"I know enough to stay out of trouble."

"You always were the one to stand back and weigh your options."

"Exactly. And don't you forget it."

"I'm not the one who needs reminding, Tommy. You're the one who told her that you play the accordion, which tells me you're the one in need of assistance."

Truer words were never spoken.

From a spot on the cabin's front porch, Tom was able to see down the hillside to the open country spread out before him. He'd made it a habit to sit on the front porch in the early evening to catch a breeze—not to catch sight of the sexy redhead next door.

She was home. Her car was parked alongside his SUV.

Not that he cared. No. He didn't need company. He liked being alone with the land. He was a solitary throwback to the old days when cowboys roamed the open range.

Tom had always felt a special affinity to the land here. From the first time he'd set foot on the ranch, something had clicked deep inside him. He'd almost forgotten until he'd come back.

But now, having spent some time here again, his appreciation returned for the rolling grass-covered hills. For the incredible number of stars in the night sky. For the gnarled branches of the live oaks that spread out above a carpet of blooming bluebonnets the color of Callie's eyes.

There she was again. Invading his thoughts.

He focused on the view before him.

Not that he'd talked about it much, but he had some fond memories of those weeks spent here as a teenager. Of rowdy rodeos trying to tame a bucking horse, of attending a square dance with a pretty girl in a blue dress, of his grandfather telling him ghost stories around the campfire.

His Polish grandmother may have secretly taught him how to play the accordion, but his Texan grandfather had taught him how to fish and tell tall tales.

That sense of audacity and valor had come in mighty handy when Tom had joined the Marine Corps.

His grandfather had not approved. In Hank King's world, Hank was commander-in-chief, a force to be obeyed.

Tom wondered if things would have been different had Hank welcomed Stan Kozlowski's marrying his only daughter instead of doing everything in his power to break them up.

Despite Hank's best efforts, none of his grandchildren had fallen in line. Threats, bribery—nothing worked. They had all become Marines. Successful Marines.

Until Tom.

Any of his brothers—even Striker, who'd been working at the oil company—could still drop and do a hundred one-handed push-ups without breaking a sweat.

But Tom couldn't.

He had no patience for any ounce of self-pity.

Regrets were different.

Not that he aimed to dwell on those. He was a Marine through and through.

That meant being unable to quit, to surrender to anything or anybody.

It meant possessing a bulldog determination in the face of adversity.

The bulldog. Now there was a mascot.

Arf was no bulldog, however. The mutt was half-asleep at his feet. Then the dog suddenly lifted his head and, in a flash, he was off, racing toward Callie's cabin.

"Come back here!" Tom ordered in a voice that crackled with authority. Any Marine within hearing distance would have stopped in his tracks.

Arf, however, totally ignored him and instead gave chase to something—something orange. Too big to be a squirrel. A yowl told Tom it was a cat. What was a cat doing out here?

"Stop that!" Callie rushed outside.

Arf immediately turned on his heels and raced back onto the porch to cower beneath Tom's chair. The cat chased right after him.

Tom waved his hands at the oncoming animal and barked out another order. "Halt!"

The cat ignored his order just as Arf had done and flew onto the porch, growling all the way before darting under a chair on the other side of the porch.

Callie raced onto the porch to defend her darling. "Bob, are you okay?"

"The name is Tom, but thanks for asking."

"I was speaking to my cat. His name is Bob."

Tom stared under the chair. "What is he, part bobcat?"

"No, he's a long-haired domestic."

"He's huge."

"It's okay, baby," she crooned, and for a moment Tom thought she was speaking to him.

But she wasn't.

"You're okay," Callie repeated in that sexy tone that put his body on high alert.

But Tom wasn't okay. He was remembering the feel of her body in his arms, of her lips beneath his, parting and allowing him entry. Of her tongue tentatively touching his.

So much for forgetting their kiss the other night.

But he was a Marine, and that meant he was an expert at self-discipline and self-control.

He just couldn't seem to control this stupid dog of his.

"Arf, stop being such a baby and come out from under there."

The dog, trembling, stuck his nose out between Tom's bare feet.

Tom reached down to pat his head reassuringly, even as his attention was distracted by the sight of Callie's bottom as she leaned over to coax her cat out from beneath the chair.

Callie was wearing a tummy-baring white tank top with hot-pink shorts that molded her curvy derriere to perfection. The lower she bent, the more creamy skin the rising hem of her shorts revealed.

Tom knew he shouldn't, but he couldn't help himself. He sat there and simply admired the view. Not of the rolling countryside but of Callie.

She had her hair piled on top of her head again. It occurred to Tom that he'd rarely seen her with it down. But he knew how silky the red strands felt against his fingers as he'd cupped her head in his hand, anchoring her when he'd intensified their kiss. Her hair had been like the softest silk. Sunlight glinted off the top of her head, creating natural highlights of golden fire.

He had to say something intelligent or he'd sit there drooling in another minute. "I didn't know you had a cat."

Well, that didn't rate very high on the conversational IQ chart, but it would have to do for the time being.

"You don't know everything about me," Callie retorted.

"Obviously not."

Tom knew enough, though. He knew she kissed as passionately as she did everything else. That Jimmy Bob's Barbecue was her favorite place to eat. That she liked tai chi and hated bullies—especially rich ones.

"Your brother said it was okay for me to bring my cat," Callie said. "He's an indoor cat."

"Not at the moment he isn't."

She wrapped her arms around her middle in a defensive pose. "He snuck out when I brought in some groceries."

"Cats need to roam free."

She immediately rounded on him. "So now you're a

specialist on the subject, are you? For your information, outdoor cats have a much shorter life span. It's a dangerous world for cats."

"It's a dangerous world for all of us."

The cat jumped onto the empty chair and started washing himself.

"Make yourself at home, why don't you?" Tom drawled.

Callie's chin lifted a notch or two. "The minute I get my cat, we're out of here."

"I was talking to your cat." Tom stood up to deliver his warning to the animal. "Listen, Bob, don't make a habit of coming over here or I won't be responsible for the consequences."

Callie immediately switched her attention from her cat to Tom.

"Nobody threatens my cat." She emphasized each word with a jab to his chest. "Got that?"

He captured her hand to prevent her from hurting herself. "For a little thing, you sure do pack a punch. I guess this temper of yours is because you're a redhead, huh?"

"I do not have a temper. On the contrary, I am known for my incredible patience."

"Really?" He sounded very doubtful.

"Yes, really."

Tom belatedly realized that he was stroking the back of her hand with his thumb. He released his hold immediately.

What had he been thinking?

Okay, scratch that question. He knew what he'd been thinking. Of her. In his arms. She had a way of getting under his skin despite his best efforts.

"A man should be able to sit on his own front porch without interruptions," he growled.

Callie scooped up Bob, who started purring so loudly you could probably hear him two counties over.

"I came here to get away from people," Tom said.

"Why would you want to get away from people?"

"I don't like them."

"All people? All over the world? That's not logical," Callie scoffed. "You haven't met everyone all over the world."

Heaven save him from logical females. Hah! Logical? Female? Talk about an oxymoron. He was getting more aggravated by the second. "You can go now."

But she showed no inclination to follow his suggestion. Instead, she seemed to derive satisfaction from having yanked his chain. "Don't give me that look. I deal with a classroom full of kindergartners. I think I can handle one crabby Marine."

"You think so, do you?"

"Absolutely." Her look dared him to prove otherwise.

"You think wrong," Tom growled, right before tugging her into his arms.

Chapter Six

Tom forgot about the cat Callie was still holding, but it leapt out of his way onto the porch railing. Callie leaned forward to catch her pet and ended up pressing her breasts against his chest.

A man could only put up with so much.

Even a Marine.

Sure he'd pulled her into his arms as a warning that he wasn't one of her kindergartners, but it was backfiring on him big time. Instead of scaring her off, he'd only intensified his desire for her.

Cupping her face with both his hands, he leaned down to kiss her.

Tom half expected her to haul off and sock him or something. Instead, for one incredible moment, she gave in and kissed him back.

Then she hauled off and socked him.

He only said "Ow" to make her think she'd made a dent in him when she really hadn't. She was a petite little thing. He forgot that sometimes because she talked big. But she was a good eight inches or more shorter than his six-foot-whatever.

"What do you think you're doing?" she demanded.

"What did you think I was doing?" he retorted, stalling for time.

"Kissing me. After you said we weren't going to do that."

"Right. It was a mistake."

"Well, gee, thanks!"

He gently took her arm when she turned away in a huff. "I didn't mean that the way it sounded."

"Do you even know what you mean?" she asked in exasperation. "Because you sure are sending mixed messages."

She had him dead to rights, which aggravated him. "You didn't have to kiss me back."

"You caught me by surprise."

"This time maybe, but not the other night."

"I was just being polite."

That really irked him. "So it was be-kind-to-an-injured-Marine night? Was that it? You were just feeling sorry for me? Kiss the poor guy because he can barely get around."

"That's not it at all!"

"No?"

"No. Why should I feel sorry for you?"

"I would think that's obvious."

"Not to me. Go on," she challenged him. "Explain to me why you are such a pitiful case."

Now she was really making him angry. "I told you that I don't want people treating me like one of the walking wounded."

Her anger lessened when she caught a glimpse of the

shadowy pain in his eyes. Tom was clearly wounded in ways beyond his physical injuries, but he refused to open up to her. "And I told you that I don't see you that way."

"So you say."

"Are you accusing me of being a liar? You sure do know how to show a girl a good time." She could see she'd floored him by teasing him. "First, you yank me into your arms and kiss me, then you call me a liar. And here you told me you knew how to be charming."

He blinked at her.

Good. She liked throwing him. Because she had the feeling that few people did. They either kowtowed to him or pitied him, as he said. And she doubted he appreciated either approach.

Not that she was saying these things to please him. But maybe she was saying them because she thought he needed to hear them. He needed someone to wake him up. To remind him there was still a big world out there. And that there was laughter to be had in it.

If he'd only give it half a chance.

She had no idea if Marines were into laughter. She only knew that she loved hearing his. The deep, rumbly sound was a bit rusty, as if it wasn't used often enough.

Not through any fault of her own. She secretly treasured those moments she'd made him laugh.

She remembered Striker once saying something about his baby brother being the fun-loving one in the family. Callie wanted to see that side of Tom, wanted him to remember what it felt like to be happy.

So she kept teasing him. "Sure, you *say* you know how to sweet-talk a girl, but I have yet to see it. Maybe I should pick up some books about it for you. I tutor at-risk kids at the local library, teaching them how to read.

While I'm there, I could get you some books if you'd like."

"What? You mean like *Courting for Dummies?*"

"Are you saying *you* could write the book on that one?"

She made him laugh. And he didn't know what to do with her. He knew what he wanted to do—tug her into his arms again and make love to her until neither one of them could think or speak. But he also knew all the reasons why he should avoid her.

She was a sexy redhead who could have her choice of men. She didn't need a torn-up Marine like him.

The next couple of days went by in a blur as Callie was consumed with getting everything done before the end of the school year. She even had to give up her morning tai chi routine because she was short on time.

It happened at the end of every school year, but it always felt like she'd never get the final report cards done or the parent-conference meetings completed.

She looked across at Adam and his mom, Sue, seated across from her. They'd already covered his work, which had been good overall, and the progress he'd made during the year. Now they'd come to how well he followed the rules.

Adam started to squirm in his seat.

"And how are you doing with the rules?" his mom asked.

"Not doing too well," Adam mumbled.

Sue frowned. "Why?"

"My blood sugar—"

"Is fine!" Sue's voice reflected her exasperation.

Adam looked around, his eyes darting from side to side. "I'm a secret agent?"

Sue shook her head. "No, that won't work, either."

"Adam has some room for improvement in following the rules," Callie said, "and I'm sure he'll do even better next year when he keeps working on that. Adam, remember what we talked about in class? About thinking about how other people feel when you say or do something that hurts them."

"Like the time Jenna pushed me off the swing and I socked her." The incident had happened at the beginning of the school year, but Adam liked focusing on it to prove how far he'd come. "I'm better now."

"Yes, you are," Callie agreed.

"Even secret agents have to follow the rules."

"That's right." Callie turned her attention to Sue. "I'm a lucky teacher to have a wonderful student like Adam in my class."

Adam beamed. "Yes, I know."

Callie and Sue exchanged looks and then laughter.

These were the moments that made it all worth it—the twelve-hour days, the work over the weekend preparing lesson plans, the money from her own pocket for the extra bulletin-board displays. Moments like this—with Adam grinning at her—were the reason Callie loved her job.

She needed to stay focused on that and not on the sexy Marine living next door to her.

But that was easier said than done. Even though she'd barely caught sight of him over the past few days, Tom remained fixed in her thoughts.

Why had he kissed her again after saying he didn't want to get involved with her? Was he trying to prove a point? If so, she sure didn't get it.

Paula dropped by her classroom after all the kids had left for the day. "Just thought you'd want to know that things seem to be working out well for Quentin."

"I'm so glad. That antibullying program really works."

"So does having a Marine by your side."

"What are you talking about?"

"Quentin's mom told me all about it. She was standing right there the other day when that hottie Marine of yours stopped by and spoke to Quentin right in front of the other kids."

"What did he say?"

"That he was proud to call Quentin a buddy of his. And he made sure the other kids heard him say that."

"He didn't threaten anyone, did he?"

Paula shook her head. "He didn't have to. The message was delivered: 'Mess with Quentin and you mess with me.'"

Callie didn't know what to say.

Paula did. "That Tom is really one of the good guys. Are you sure you won't reconsider your no-rich-guys policy? I really think that if anyone deserves a chance, it's Tom."

"He told me that he's not interested in starting anything with me. You can't get much more blunt than that."

"When did he say that?"

"After he kissed me the first time."

"The first time?" Paula immediately picked up on that. "Which means he's kissed you more than once. And you didn't say a word. Shame on you! I'm your friend. You're supposed to tell me this stuff."

"It's been kind of busy around here lately in case you haven't noticed."

"Things are never too busy that we can't talk about men—what's wrong with them, how we can improve them, how they aggravate us and how they make our knees weak."

Tom certainly did that, all right. Made her knees go weak and her heart all fluttery.

"So tell me more about this kiss," Paula said.

"There's nothing to tell."

"Is he a good kisser?"

Callie hurried to the classroom door and looked both ways down the hallway before returning and closing the door behind her. No way would she risk Tom walking in on this conversation as he had the other day.

"Oh yeah, he's incredibly good." She giggled and then frowned. "Listen to me, I sound like a teenager. The man is sapping my brain cells."

"Ah, sounds like love to me."

"No, it doesn't!" Callie vehemently denied. "That's not a possibility."

"Why not? Because he's rich?"

"For a lot of reasons. That's one of them. The fact that he doesn't want to get involved is another biggie."

"Yet he keeps kissing you. As if he can't help himself, huh? He just can't resist you."

"Oh please! He's had plenty of women falling at his feet, I'm sure. Maybe not as many since he was hurt, but that's just because he hasn't been out much."

"You don't think some women would be turned off by his injuries."

"If they are, they're idiots!" Callie stated vehemently.

"Sounds like you're falling for him."

"His brother Striker is my grandmother's boss."

Paula nodded. "Yeah, I know. You already told me that. I never did understand why that was a problem, though."

"It would make things awkward. Getting involved with the boss or anyone in his family is problematic."

"No one in his family is *your* boss."

"I don't want to do anything that would endanger my grandmother's position with King Oil."

"You really think getting involved with Tom would do that?"

"I'm not willing to take the risk."

"Ah, now that sounds like the real reason."

"What do you mean?" Callie said.

"The real reason you don't want to fall for Tom is that you're not willing to take a risk. You don't want to risk having your heart broken."

"Who does?"

"Yeah, but *you* are especially cautious about it."

Callie shrugged. "Maybe I've had reason to be."

"Want to tell me about it?"

"The inner geek in me distrusts men who are swayed by a woman's outward appearance. They want someone who looks good. They don't want to bother getting to know you. I don't like that. I have opinions and I voice them."

"You think Tom is looking for some kind of pretty trophy wife?"

"I don't think he's looking for a wife at all. He's as good as told me that."

"Yet he keeps kissing you," Paula pointed out.

"It was only two times."

"Do you think he's going around kissing other women?"

"I don't think so, but I have no way of knowing for sure."

"If you're waiting until you know for sure, you may be waiting forever. Sometimes you have to have faith."

"I'm not good at that," Callie quietly admitted. "I had faith that my mom would recover after the fire, but she didn't. She died."

"And when she died, your faith in happy endings died with her?"

"Maybe." Callie hadn't talked about this with anyone. She hadn't even consciously thought about it until now. Until Paula had confronted her. "I really don't want to talk about it anymore."

"Okay." Paula rubbed Callie's shoulder reassuringly. "We don't have to talk about it anymore. Everything will be okay."

Called blinked away a sudden rush of tears, triggering the unexpected memory of her third-grade teacher telling her, *They pick on you because you're weak.*

Which made Callie think at the time that it was all *her* fault, that she'd somehow provoked the attacks and deserved them.

As an adult, she knew that was horse manure.

"It's just that bullies get to me," she explained with a wobbly smile.

"I wasn't trying to bully you," Paula denied.

"No, I didn't mean you." She gave Paula a quick hug. "I was thinking of Quentin and those kids who bullied him. He's not alone, unfortunately. Five million elementary and middle-school students in the U.S. are bullied each year. Every day, bullies' cruel teasing makes 160,000 fearful kids skip school."

"Which is why we kick off each new school year with an assembly and follow-up programs promoting politeness and civility throughout the year. And the bullying-prevention lessons you have in the kindergarten curriculum certainly get things started on the right track."

"I just wish there was more I could do."

"You're doing plenty. That new buddy-mentor program you created is being tested at several other area schools. In your spare time, you set up the entire program for other teachers to follow. And you wrote that grant that got us more money for additional antibullying programs this year."

"I know, but..."

"The fact that you were a victim of bullying yourself makes this a hot button issue for you."

"School was no piece of cake," Callie said.

"I get that. You have reasons for being distrustful. All I'm saying is that some things and some people are worth taking a risk on. And I think this Marine of yours is one of them."

That sounded all well and good, but Tom wasn't her Marine. He was his own man. One who didn't want to get involved with her. And Callie would do well to remember that fact.

"I can read now!" José proudly proclaimed. He was one of her star pupils in the small reading group for at-risk kids and their moms that she tutored at the local public library on Saturday mornings.

"Yes, you can."

"My mom can read, too!"

"Yes, she can." The literacy program was intended to bring moms and kids together through books, teaching both the parent and the child at the same time.

"One day, we'll read all the books in the library!" José said.

His mother, Rosaria, laughed. "You have big dreams, niño."

"Big dreams are good," Callie told her with a smile.

After the session was over, she tidied up the books she'd taken off the shelves. She had a pile in her arms, ready to reshelve, when a man's voice stopped her in her tracks.

Turning, she saw that Tom was standing at the

adult circulation desk, speaking to one of the librarians there.

Looking up, he saw her. A minute later, he approached her, and she saw that his limp was a little less noticeable today than it had been in the past. He wasn't using his cane. Because he no longer needed it or because he was too proud to use it?

He looked entirely too good in khaki shorts and a sleeveless navy-blue T-shirt.

"Were you asking her where to find *Courting for Dummies?*" she teased him.

"No, I came to pick up some books for Kate."

"Aren't you going to ask me what I'm doing here?"

"No. We seem to do that entirely too much."

"Oh."

Tom watched her reaction. She looked all fresh and perky in a purple top and jeans that covered her like a second skin. A hint of bare skin showed near her midriff. She clutched a pile of books to her chest as if holding onto a life jacket. "So what are you doing here?" he finally asked.

"I do volunteer work on Saturdays."

He raised an eyebrow. "Shelving books?"

"Working with kids and moms, teaching them both how to read."

"A worthy cause."

"I think so."

"I noticed that you haven't been doing your workout routine in the mornings. Did Arf scare you off?"

"No, he's a sweetie."

Tom appeared offended. "He's not a poodle."

"I didn't say he was. He's a big bruiser with a heart of gold. Does that sound better?"

"Affirmative."

"Well, he's not the reason I haven't been practicing my tai chi. Next week is the last week of school and I've been really busy."

"Me, too."

"I'm sorry that Bob scared Arf the other day."

"A big bruiser like Arf wouldn't be afraid of a monster cat like yours. I figured out later that he was under my chair because he was trying to protect his master."

"From the monster cat."

"Yeah."

"Brave of him."

"I thought so. Gave him extra doggy treats that night."

"Lucky Arf."

She caught his gaze and they shared a smile.

Callie felt all warm and glowing inside. She had an almost overwhelming urge to reach out and cup his cheek and the fading scar with her hand. She tightened her hold on the books to stop herself from doing something she'd regret.

"So how have things been going?" she asked.

"Great. Any more problems with Quentin and the bullies?"

"No. I heard through the grapevine that you helped Quentin out."

Tom just shrugged as if he had no knowledge of this.

"That was kind of you."

"First, my dog is a sweetie, and now I'm kind." He sounded a tad disgusted.

"You're a big bruiser with a heart of gold, just like your big bruiser dog. Is that better?"

"Affirmative."

She loved sharing smiles with him.

This could become addictive.

Danger zone, Callie Murphy, a little voice in her head warned.

We're just friends having a polite conversation, her logical side responded.

Then why are your palms all sweaty? And your heartbeat accelerated?

She was experiencing all the clichés associated with infatuation.

Was Tom? Were his palms sweaty? His heartbeat accelerated? She doubted it. He was a war-tested Marine. Out of her league.

"I, uh, I didn't expect to see you here," she said.

"Marines do know how to read, you know. In fact, the Marine Corps is the only branch of the armed forces that has a reading list of books for all ranks to read and discuss."

"I didn't know that."

"There's a lot you don't know about me."

"Totally true," she acknowledged.

"Although you do know about the accordion thing." He looked around and lowered his voice. "And, speaking of that, I've been meaning to ask you not to say anything about it to Striker or anyone else."

"Why not?"

"It's not something I go around bragging about."

"Unlike, say, being good at football or kissing?"

"Yeah, that's right."

"Don't worry," she reassured him. "I'll keep your secret." After all, she had a few secrets of her own. Not the least of which were her increasing feelings for a certain wounded warrior.

Chapter Seven

The phone was ringing when Callie returned from volunteering at the library and running errands. She dumped her bag of groceries on the round oak table and answered it.

"Hey, sweetie." Tex's booming voice came through loud and clear. "How ya doin'?"

"I'm doing fine, Gran. How are things with you?"

"Can't complain. You all settled in at the cabin now?"

"Yes." Callie looked around. She'd managed to make the place look like hers despite the fact that it was furnished and most of her furniture was in storage. But she'd added a few touches, like the ultrasoft, plum-colored microfiber throw tossed over the edge of the otherwise masculine brown leather couch. And through the open bedroom door, she could see the feminine, antique floral quilt, with its intricate stitching and scalloped edges. The lacy sheet set on the bed added to the romantic feel of the room.

"That Marine next door giving you any grief?" Tex demanded.

Callie turned her back on her bedroom. No point inviting images of Tom sprawled out on her sheets. "No."

"Glad to hear it. You have any trouble, you come to me, you hear?"

"I will."

"School year's almost over, isn't it?"

"That's right."

"You hear anything new about the town house?"

"No."

"Not real talkative today, are you?"

"I just got in. I was out getting groceries and running some errands."

And running into Tom at the library.

"Don't you do your tutoring on Saturdays?"

"That's right. José and his mom graduated today. They are both reading."

"Have I told you how proud I am of you, hon?"

"Yes, Gran."

"Proud as a peacock in full bloom."

"Or a pup with a new collar," Callie said with a laugh.

"I taught you well."

"Of course you did."

"You wouldn't do anything foolish."

"Like jumping in a river to get out of the rain?" That had been a favorite expression of her grandmother's while Callie was in school.

"Like getting your heart broken by that mighty good-looking baby brother of Striker's."

"I won't do anything that foolish."

"Good. That makes me happier than a raccoon—"

"In a cornfield," Callie completed for her. "You

know, Gran, you've used more Texas sayings in the past two minutes than you usually use in a week. What's up?"

"It's that Wally Joyner next door," Tex grumbled.

Wally was a retiree, a former accountant who collected stamps for a hobby and generally got on Tex's nerves. "What's he done now?"

"Asked me out. On a date. Can you imagine the nerve?"

"What did you say?"

"I told him what he could do with his invitation."

"Why did you do that?"

"He only asked me out because Gladys across the street turned him down."

"Who told you that?"

"Gladys did."

Callie sighed. "You know, Gladys doesn't always tell the truth. Remember that time she said that she was related to Tom Cruise?"

"Yes."

"That was a lie. And what about the time she said that she was a former Miss Texas?"

"Okay, but she was telling the truth about Wally."

"How do you know?"

"Because I asked him," Tex said.

"And he said that he was only asking you out because Gladys turned him down?"

"Not exactly."

"What exactly did he say?"

"That I wasn't the first woman who came to mind for him to take to the condo association picnic tomorrow."

"Did you ask who the first woman was?"

"He said it was his daughter."

"I'm more inclined to believe Wally than Gladys.

You thought he was rather dashing when he first moved in a year ago."

"That was before I realized he was a Casanova, asking all the women in the complex out."

"So now what are you going to do?"

"Go to that picnic tomorrow looking as pretty as a field of bluebonnets. I even bought a new outfit. That should show Wally."

"Knock his socks off, huh?"

"Don't you worry about Wally. I can take care of him. You just take care of yourself, you hear?"

Callie heard her all right. Tex had the sort of voice one didn't soon forget.

When the phone rang a short while later, Callie thought it was Tex with more advice. Instead, it was Striker's wife, Kate.

"I've been meaning to call and see how you're settling in," Kate said. "I really should have stopped by myself, but there's so much to do yet before the baby comes…."

"Don't worry," Callie reassured her. "I'm doing fine."

"Really?"

"Yes, really. Why? You don't sound all that convinced."

"It's just that I know that initially Tom wasn't really thrilled at the idea of having company."

"I'm not company."

"A neighbor then."

Callie's stomach sank. "If my being here is going to cause trouble—"

"No, you don't understand," Kate interrupted her. "I'm thrilled that you're here. And relieved."

"Why is that?"

"Because I don't trust Tom to look after himself. And I've been nagging him so long he doesn't listen to me anymore. He just tells me what he thinks I want to hear."

"He wouldn't be the first guy to pull that stunt."

Kate laughed. "No, he wouldn't. Listen, how would you like to stop by the house for dinner sometime?"

"Oh, I couldn't. You've already got enough to do…."

"We have a cook. She's a talented magician where food is concerned. It wouldn't be anything formal. Just a casual meal next to the pool. Bring a suit. How does tomorrow sound? Unless you have plans?"

"No, no plans." Other than putting in several hours of working on her students' end-of-year files.

"Good. Come early and swim beforehand. Build up an appetite. And thanks for keeping an eye on Tom for me. Make sure the man eats, would you?" Kate added before saying goodbye.

Make sure the man eats? How was Callie supposed to do that when he didn't want her around?

She could just imagine the reception she'd get if she walked over to his cabin and knocked on his door to ask him what he was having for dinner tonight.

That would go over real big, she was sure.

No, she should mind her own business.

But what if Tom was neglecting his meals because he was in pain? Now that she thought about it, he had seemed a little thinner at the library earlier today. Was anyone else checking up on him, making sure he ate?

Maybe everyone thought that Callie was looking after Tom.

If that was the game plan, someone should have warned her ahead of time.

Not that Tom seemed like he needed or wanted anyone hovering over him. He'd told her in no uncertain terms that one of the reasons he liked her was because she didn't treat him like an invalid.

She should mind her own business. She should leave him alone. She should fix her own dinner.

She did, and to her utter amazement, the recipe for lasagna turned out delicious. So delicious that she felt guilty not sharing it.

In fact, Callie was so excited with her success that she wrapped up a plate and rushed right over to Tom's cabin.

She wasn't checking up on him, she was declaring her power as a cooking diva! Who knew she had such powers? They rarely showed up when called upon. This was too momentous an occasion not to share.

Tom yanked the door open with the irritation he'd shown the first time she'd shown up unannounced. She refused to allow the scowl on his face to ruin her excitement. "You have to try this!"

"What?"

"You have to eat this. It's wonderful." She whipped the plastic wrap off the plate and headed for the coffee table in front of the couch. "Hurry, before it gets cold."

"I'm not hungr—"

She stuck a forkful into his mouth.

Tom glared at her. He quickly chewed and then swallowed.

"I'm not a kid who needs feeding," he growled.

"I know that. Here, have some more." She handed him the fork. "I made this. From scratch!"

He took another forkful, chewed, then became thoughtful. "It's good. *Really* good."

"I know. Isn't it amazing? That's why I had to come over here."

"I thought you said you couldn't cook."

"I know. I can't believe it turned out so good!"

"You seem surprised."

"I am. Totally. And psyched. I feel all-powerful! I mean, it does taste great, doesn't it? You're not just being polite, right? What am I thinking? Of course you're not. You're not into polite."

"Gee, thanks."

"You know what I mean. You wouldn't say something you didn't mean just to be—"

"Polite."

"Right."

"Marines are trained to be polite."

"But to be honest, right? Not to lie. So you wouldn't lie and tell me it was good if it wasn't."

"What happened to the confident culinary virtuoso from a moment ago?"

"I guess I'm not much better at being a virtuoso than I was at being a simpering sweetie. I still can't believe I made this!"

"Next thing you know, you'll be whipping up pies and soufflés."

"Don't hold your breath," she said. "The last pie I made was a disaster. I'm generally pretty good at baking cookies, though. From scratch. Chocolate chip are my specialty."

Tom remembered her face when she'd eaten that wicked brownie at the restaurant. She had a similar glow on her face now. Her blue eyes were sparkling with excitement and joy. Her lips were curved up in a smile that radiated her enthusiasm.

"I didn't mean to just burst in on you like this," Callie added. "I just got carried away for a minute."

He'd like to carry her away, sweep her up into his

arms, take her into his bedroom and peel away the cute little tank top she was wearing. But with his injuries, he could no more pick her up than he could fly to the moon.

"I should have called first," she said, "but then everything would have gotten cold."

Tom was so hot that he couldn't imagine anything getting cold. He only had to look at her and he was shaken up. Just like that first night when she'd shown up unannounced on his doorstep. You'd have thought that he'd have gotten over whatever it was that had caught his attention by now.

But the more time he spent with her, the more intrigued he was with her.

"Sit down and eat," she told him.

"A Marine doesn't sit while a woman stands."

"Fine, then I'll sit, too."

She sat on the end of the couch, giving him plenty of room. She was just about bouncing up and down on that curvaceous bottom of hers, draped in those shorts he'd found so sexy the last time he'd seen her wearing them, when she'd come after her cat.

He sat down, careful to keep some distance between them. He was wearing gym shorts and a sleeveless T-shirt. He watched to see her reaction to the scars on his leg.

She didn't look away in horror or scoot away from him. Instead she seemed focused on his reaction to the food she'd made.

When she finally did look around, it was to search for Arf. "Where's your dog?"

"Sleeping. He's pretty lazy."

"In Texas, we'd say he has to lean against a fence to bark."

"Arf doesn't bark much. That's why I gave him that name."

As they talked more about the foibles of pet ownership, time passed so quickly that Tom didn't even realize he'd cleaned his plate until he looked down and noticed it was empty.

Callie stood. "Well, I guess I should be going. Thanks for sampling my masterpiece. No, don't get up—"

But of course he did. "Thanks for bringing it over."

Arf made a grand appearance, stretching out in a huge yawn before trotting over to jump onto the couch that Callie and Tom had just abandoned.

The dog rolled onto his back, a clear indication that he wanted his tummy rubbed. Callie laughed and readily obliged.

"I'm glad he doesn't hold a grudge against me for having Bob scare him the other day," she said.

"As I told you before, he was protecting me."

"Right. What a big, brave boy you are," Callie crooned to an adoring Arf.

"Rub his stomach and he's anybody's buddy."

Callie shot Tom a teasing look. "What's the matter? Are you jealous?"

Tom instantly got an image of Callie running her fingers over his stomach. His body tightened in an immediate reaction.

He'd faced plenty of tough situations as a Marine, but this woman had the ability to get to him in ways he hadn't experienced before, and he didn't know how to defend himself against her. Just when he thought he had the situation under control, she'd do or say something that would get him all fired up again.

In any other female, he'd suspect she was doing it

on purpose, as some sort of plan to undermine the walls he'd erected.

The bottom line was that he needed to stick to his game plan here and not get distracted by a sexy kindergarten teacher who drove him to distraction.

His focus was on regaining his position with the Marine Corps. Period. End of discussion.

Callie floated peacefully. Kate had invited her to take a late Sunday afternoon swim, assuring her that she'd be on her own. Callie had worn her black halter-top swimsuit beneath her shorts. The day was sunny and muggy, making the cool water a delight.

Kate and Striker had redone the pool area here at Westwind Ranch since the last time Callie had visited—during the King Oil company picnic last year.

The new version looked like something out of a magazine, defined by cream-colored cut-stone coping. The sudden image of synchronized swimmers came to mind, making Callie grin and daintily lift one leg in her own imitation of one of their routines.

"Nice form," Tom drawled.

Startled, Callie gulped in a mouthful of chlorinated water and ended up sputtering. Grabbing hold of the edge of the pool with one hand, she wiped the water from her eyes with the other.

Tom stood there, right above her.

It wasn't the first time she'd seen him without a shirt. She recalled thinking that his shoulders were as wide as a tank, but now she noticed the muscular delineations of his chest and washboard abs. No tank had ever looked so good.

In the raking sunlight, she saw the fading scars on

his chest and side, their slightly raised white markings visible against his otherwise-tanned body.

Despite his injuries, he held himself with an authority that came from being a Marine.

His suit wasn't those abbreviated Speedo swim trunks but was perfectly respectable. Her thoughts weren't.

"We meet again," he drawled.

"Kate invited me. She said I'd have the pool to myself."

"It's a big pool. There's room enough for both of us."

"No, that's okay. I'll get out of your way." Since she was at the shallow end of the pool, Callie bounced her way through the water over to the steps.

"You don't have to do that."

She ignored his comment and reached for a towel she'd left on one of the chairs, intending to wrap it around her waist. Instead, she bumped into his warm hand as he held the towel for her.

The all-too-familiar zing of sexual awareness hummed up her arm.

Her eyes met his. Was she the only one who felt the electricity?

She wished she could read his thoughts, but there was no deciphering what might be in the shadow of his gaze.

Stepping away from her, Tom headed straight for the deep end of the pool. No shallows for him.

She watched him as he started swimming laps with the determination of someone who was either trying to break a world record or outdistance demons.

She wasn't able to look away. Heat consumed her as she saw the ripple of his muscles.

Wanting to cool off, Callie headed for the spa, adjacent to the pool and separated from it by a cascading rocky waterfall. She hoped its healing water therapy would calm her churning emotions.

The jets felt good, gradually relaxing her tense body. She leaned back, resting her head along the edge of the spa.

Don't get used to all this pampering, she sternly ordered her hedonistic self. You don't really belong in a place like this.

She was just a teacher trying to make her paycheck stretch enough to pay all her bills and still have enough to put a little away for her emergency fund. She wasn't born into this lifestyle the way Kate was.

And, okay, so Tom didn't grow up wealthy, but he had money now.

"He has money. You don't," she muttered.

"Is that your way of telling me that you're after my money?" Tom asked from beside the spa.

Startled, Callie slipped under the water again. For a second, she wished she could stay down there.

He pulled her up to the surface and, in doing so, loosened the halter top of her swimsuit. She didn't realize it until she felt the material slipping off her neck. She immediately put both hands on her breasts, clamping the material in place.

"Need a hand?" he drawled.

"No!" she growled.

"Are you sure?"

"Positive."

Any one of her students could have told Tom that when Ms. Murphy used that voice it meant you were in *big* trouble. Up to your armpits in alligators.

But the Marine showed no signs of backing away. "I'd be more than glad to help."

"You've done too much already."

"What did I do?"

"Startled me." Callie carefully slid her hands up and repositioned the ties back in place. But her wet fingers were having a hard time getting it refastened.

Tom didn't help matters any by joining her in the relatively small confines of the spa. There might have been room for them both in the large pool but not in this cozy environment.

She was definitely in hot water here.

He leaned closer.

"Do *not* help me," she warned him.

"I was just reaching for a drink." He tugged on a rock and opened a tiny fridge camouflaged in the rockface. "Want one?"

Her hands were full at the moment, so she shook her head. That almost dislodged the left tie again.

Since this was his brother's spa on his family's ranch, she could hardly ask him to leave. And she couldn't get up without her swimsuit being refastened.

"A gentleman would look away," she informed him.

"A lady would accept a gentleman's offer to help," he retorted.

She glared at him. "Are you saying I'm not a lady?"

"Are you saying I'm not a gentleman?" he countered.

She wanted to but didn't.

"What's the matter?" he teased. "Bobcat got your tongue?"

She remained stubbornly silent.

"You're being ridiculous," he added.

"I had no way of knowing this suit would do this!"

"I meant you not letting me help you."

"I'd rather handle this myself."

Wrong phrase to use.

To give him credit, Tom didn't say he'd like to handle her. He didn't have to say the words aloud. His eloquently heated gaze said it for him.

Of course, with him looking at her that way, she was all thumbs. She tried closing her eyes and focusing on what she was doing, but that didn't help, either.

She opened her eyes and found herself staring right at him. He'd lifted a bottle of beer to his lips, holding it around the neck the way any good Texan would. She stupidly said, "Doing that keeps the bottle cold because the heat of your hand won't warm it up."

The image of the heat of his hand warming her up did nothing to make her battle with the ties of her swimsuit any easier. Indeed, she paused momentarily, distracted by the slide of his Adam's apple as he swallowed before speaking.

"What are you talking about?" Tom said.

Feeling like an idiot, she said, "Longnecks. The way you were drinking your beer."

There was a moment of silence, during which she finally got her stupid suit fastened. She even cautiously tugged on it to make sure it would stay in place this time.

"So what did you mean earlier?" Tom asked.

"Earlier?"

"Yeah, when you were talking to yourself about him having money and you not."

Callie's mind went blank. She was intelligent. She should have been thinking of an answer to that question while trying to redo her swimsuit.

But the fear of going topless right before his eyes had momentarily robbed her of her sanity. That plus the fact that he was sitting within arm's reach of her and looking entirely too good.

"I'm not after your money," she blurted out.

"You're not?"

"No way," she said emphatically.

"Yeah, well I can see where a banged-up Marine might not be worth the money," he noted bitterly.

"That's not the reason."

There was a new edginess in his gaze now. "Did Kate set this up?"

"What do you mean?"

"I mean she's behind this, isn't she? Sending you over to check up on me last night."

"She's worried about you."

Wrong thing to say. His eyes turned dark and cool. "I don't need looking after like some snot-nosed little kid."

With that declaration, he abruptly got up and left.

Callie stayed in the spa as long as she could, but her fingers and toes were starting to resemble prunes. Surely she'd given Tom enough time to cool down and could explain that she hadn't been checking up on him. Not really.

As she approached the sliding doors leading to the house, she heard Tom's voice. "No more matchmaking, Kate. If I want a woman, I'll go get one. Stop throwing Callie at me."

Appalled, Callie stood frozen just inside the threshold. Humiliation held her in its grip as his angry words impaled themselves into her heart.

Callie saw the horrified expression on Kate's face. Apparently, Tom saw it, too, because he turned to face Callie.

Callie couldn't bear to look at him, other than to vaguely notice that he'd put more clothes on.

Instead, she looked down, focusing her attention on

the sarong she'd wrapped around her waist. Yes, it was fastened right. Good. And she had her tote bag with her shorts in it. Check. All belongings accounted for.

"I didn't mean for you to overhear that," Tom said.

"I wasn't eavesdropping," Callie said with quiet dignity. "I just came inside to tell you that I got a call from Tex on my cellphone and something has come up. I have to leave. I'm sorry." With those words, her throat closed up.

Feeling her eyes burn with the threat of tears, Callie quickly walked out before she made a fool of herself.

Chapter Eight

"Nice going, bro." Striker glared at Tom. "I walk in just in time to hear you making a donkey's behind of yourself."

Tom glared right back. "It is not my fault she had to leave." Saying the words didn't help convince him that they were true, however.

"Of course it's your fault. Tex never calls people on their cellphones. She can't stand the things. Callie lit out of here as if she were on fire because of you."

Swearing under his breath and feeling lower than pond scum, Tom went after Callie. He hadn't meant to hurt her. He'd been in a rotten mood all day and had taken his frustration out on her.

By the time he reached the front door, she'd already reached her car. She could move faster than he could. But he was determined to catch her, despite the fact that his knee was giving him grief.

"Hold on a second!" He grabbed hold of the car door, as much to support himself as to make her stay.

She refused to look directly at him. "I have to go."

"I'm sorry you heard that."

"It's no big deal." She stubbornly kept her gaze on an invisible point just above his right shoulder.

"I shouldn't have said what I did." He turned on all the charm he once possessed. At one time, he'd known how to talk to women. Even how to sweet-talk them. "Please, come back inside."

Callie turned to toss her bag into her car before pivoting to face him. Anger flared in her vivid blue eyes. "Women aren't like loaves of bread, you know!"

"What?"

"You don't pick one up at the grocery store like a loaf of bread. Or maybe somebody like you does."

"What do you mean somebody like me?"

"Rich. Thinking you can buy whatever you want. A stripper. A woman."

He stiffened. "Meaning a woman wouldn't want to be with me if I didn't pay her?"

"That's not what I meant at all. Don't try to turn this around and make yourself out to be the victim here."

"I am *not* a victim." His voice was harsh. "I'm a Marine."

"Then act like one!"

Her words hit him in the gut.

"So have you two settled your differences yet?" Striker shouted from the open front door.

"Go away," Tom growled at him. "We're busy."

For once, Striker didn't argue.

"I shouldn't have said what I just did," Callie noted stiffly.

"Why not? You're right."

She blinked. "I am?"

"Affirmative. I haven't been in the best of moods

lately and I've taken it out on you. I apologize for that. You deserve better. A Marine always owns up to his mistakes."

Callie was speechless. She never expected Tom to admit he was wrong. "I thought Marines were never wrong."

"It happens on extremely rare occasions. What I said was completely out of line."

Studying his expression, she saw the regret reflected in his eyes. She saw it because he *let* her see. His earlier attempt at charm was replaced with reality as he lowered his defenses enough to allow her closer.

Because he was right. She did deserve better.

"Kate didn't tell me you were going to be here," Callie felt compelled to say.

"Ditto. But that doesn't mean we can't both enjoy ourselves while we're here. Do you accept my apology?"

Callie nodded. "Yes."

"Then prove it."

"What do you mean?"

"Come back inside and stay for dinner like Kate originally planned. Come on. My oldest brother might be a pain in the butt sometimes, but he does grill a mighty fine steak. What do you say? Do you think Tex can wait a little longer for you?"

She paused, not sure what to do.

"Please stay, Callie. *Please.*" His gruff voice did it. Broke through her defenses and made her reluctantly give in.

"Okay, but I'll have to leave right after we eat."

"Fair enough."

Tom escorted her back toward the house. With him beside her, Callie was suddenly even more aware of the luxury of Westwind Ranch. It was definitely more mansion than mere house.

The white pillars standing guard on either side of the front door made the place look more like the White House than a western ranch.

Inside, expensive Oriental rugs muffled the sound of their footsteps. Her daisy-adorned flip-flops looked out of place in such plush surroundings.

A large portrait of Tom's grandfather Hank King, gazing out at the world as if daring anyone to mess with him, hung in the two-story-high foyer.

"Striker keeps threatening to take that painting down, but Kate reminds him that Granddad brought the two of them together."

Callie nodded. She'd heard the story. Multimillionaire oilman Hank King had left his empire to his eldest grandson, Striker, with the provision that he run the company for at least two months. Striker hadn't wanted to comply, and he certainly hadn't looked forward to working with Kate as the executor of his grandfather's will.

"Did *you* get along with your grandfather?" Callie asked.

"I don't know if *get along* is the right term to use. He'd mellowed a bit by the time I spent my summer here at the ranch. All of us spent a few weeks here at some point or another during our teen years. I was sixteen. I learned a lot. How to repair a barbed wire fence, how to tie a fly lure. And I learned that I wanted to be a Marine, much to Granddad's dismay."

"Did you come here with your twin brother?"

"Yeah. I liked it better than Steve did. Probably because I was more into following rules and he was more into breaking them."

"Is that still the case?"

A shadow passed over his face. "No."

Callie had the feeling that Tom was the one who'd changed, but she didn't want to press him about it.

Instead, she went along as he took her arm and led her toward the great room at the back of the house, furnished in western style with comfy brown leather couches and lodgepole pine tables and lamps. "It turns out Callie can stay for dinner after all," he told Striker and Kate.

Callie had been too upset when she'd rushed out earlier to even register Striker's presence. Wearing one of his customary Hawaiian shirts with khaki shorts, Striker welcomed her return with a smile.

His wife was more expressive.

"I'm so glad." Kate rushed forward to give her an enthusiastic hug, erasing Callie's second thoughts about returning. "There's entirely too much testosterone around here. I'm so glad this little one is a girl." She patted her large tummy.

"You already know the baby's sex?" Callie said.

Kate nodded. "I wanted to know what color to paint the nursery."

"She has control issues," Striker stated with a grin.

"Look who's talking," Kate retorted. "Ignore everything the men say," she told Callie. "They're a different species. Incapable of asking for directions or reading instructions. Unable to locate socks."

"Watch out," Striker warned Tom with a grin. "They've started man bashing."

Tom knew his oldest brother had a great marriage. He didn't always know how Kate put up with him, but then she was pretty special.

Callie was pretty special, too.

And that made him very uneasy.

"Be nice. I'm pregnant," Kate said to her husband.

"Yeah, I noticed that," Striker replied. "Hey, did I tell you that we're ahead in the Kozlowski baby lottery? We're the odds-on favorite to have the baby before Ben and Ellie have theirs."

"We?" Kate lifted a mocking eyebrow. "*I'm* the one who goes into labor."

"It's a joint mission," Striker declared. "In fact, I was talking to Ben the other day and he said that he has sympathy cravings."

"He craves sympathy?" Tom found that hard to believe. Sure, Ben was the caretaker in the family, but he was also a Marine.

"No, bonehead." Striker grabbed a napkin off the pine sideboard and crumpled it before tossing it at Tom, who calmly sidestepped it. "I mean that he was eating weird stuff like rolled-up ham with chocolate syrup inside. And peanut-butter-and-pickle sandwiches."

"That's not weird," Tom scoffed. "Marines like mixing things up. They like getting creative with MREs."

"MREs are meals ready to eat," Striker translated for Callie's benefit. "You haven't lived until you've had Tabasco sauce, peanut butter and M&M's candy mixed in with chicken à la king."

"And you had the nerve to make a face at me when I cooked M&M's on my frozen pizza," Kate said. "And put black olives on my cheesecake. And guacamole on cornflakes. And made canned tuna with chopped-up strawberries and pickles all mixed together."

"Now that's just nasty," Striker maintained.

"Ellie and I both seem to be craving lots of ice, too," Kate added. She pointed to a cup she had set on a nearby table in the great room. "I'm always crunching on ice."

"Even in the middle of the night sometimes." Striker rolled his eyes. "And when a pregnant woman craves something, man, watch out. She's gotta have it *now!* And she's worse than a drill sergeant at demanding that she get it."

"That's the only language you Marines understand," Kate said. "And it's not just weird stuff I crave. It's also stuff like pistachio pudding. Yummy! I just made some for dessert."

"Don't be surprised if she eats it all herself," Striker warned them.

Kate took a page out of his book and tossed a crumpled-up cocktail napkin at her husband. "Just for that, you don't get any."

"Fine by me. By the way, how's that surprise party coming along?" Striker asked Kate.

She blinked. "What surprise party?"

"You're speaking to a former Force Recon Marine, hon." Striker placed an arm around Kate's shoulders. "You're not gonna be able to con me. That skunk just ain't gonna mate."

Kate lifted her chin in the air and loftily informed him, "I have no idea what you're talking about."

Striker just grinned. "Sure."

She narrowed her eyes at him. "No, really."

"Nice try, hon." He kissed her cheek. "Well, I better go out and check those steaks on the grill."

The minute he was outside, Tom spoke first. "He knows."

"No, he doesn't." Kate was adamant. "He *suspects* maybe. Did you tell him anything?"

Tom shook his head. "No way."

"Then why does he suspect anything?"

Tom shrugged. "Like Striker said, he's a former

Force Recon Marine. Hard to pull anything over on him."

"Yes, but this party isn't even on his birthday," Kate pointed out. "Or near it, for that matter."

"A nice twist," Tom agreed.

"So going back to my original question, who slipped up?"

Tom replied, "I have no idea, counselor. It wasn't me."

Kate blinked away sudden tears.

Alarmed, Tom said, "You're not going to get hormonal on me, are you?"

Her tears were replaced by anger. "What do you know about me being hormonal?"

"Uh, nothing?"

"Try again. What did Striker tell you?" Kate moved in on him.

"Nothing." Tom was pleased with how emphatically he'd said that.

"Swear on your honor as a Marine."

Shoot, she had him there. "I can't answer on the grounds that I might incriminate myself."

Kate yelled out the open French doors at Striker. "Did you tell your brother I'm hormonal?"

A second later, Striker was in the room. "What did you say to her?" Striker glared at Tom.

"I have no idea."

"You men always stick together." Kate wiped away more tears. "Especially you *Marine* men."

"She doesn't sound too happy about that," Tom noted.

"Brilliant deduction, Einstein." Turning to his wife, Striker said, "Now, honey—"

"Don't use that tone of voice with me," she warned him.

"Whatever my brother said to make you cry—"

"He—" Kate gulped "—he called me counselor."

"The low-down dog," Striker growled.

Kate sniffed and wiped her damp cheeks. "It just made me miss my work."

Striker's expression became confused. "But you were the one who decided you wanted to stay home now with the new baby coming and all."

"I know." Kate put her hands on her hips before waving them in the air. "I didn't say it was logical. I don't always have to be logical, you know."

"Affirmative. No need to always be logical. Got that?" Striker turned to growl at Tom.

"Absolutely."

"Now can we cut out the dramatics and just eat?" Striker said.

As suddenly as she'd started crying, Kate started laughing and ended up in her husband's arms.

Callie's throat tightened at the love displayed on both Striker's and Kate's faces. She wondered what it would be like to have a man look at her that way, to be part of such a powerful emotional partnership.

"Are they always like that?" Callie whispered to Tom.

"No, of course not." Tom paused. "Sometimes they're worse."

"I heard that," Kate noted. "And I just heard our son, Sean." She pointed to a child monitor on the side table. "He must be up from his nap."

"Probably heard his mother bellowing at his dad," Striker said.

"I would never do such a thing," Kate retorted. "You must be imagining things."

"I had witnesses," Striker reminded her before turning to his brother. "Right?"

Tom shook his head. "I have no idea what you're talking about. I heard no bellowing. What about you, Callie? Did you hear any bellowing?"

Callie shook her head.

The rest of dinner was surprisingly enjoyable and easygoing, given the earlier dramatics. The steaks were as delicious as Tom had promised. Ditto for the baked potatoes and the heirloom-tomato salad.

As Callie watched the interaction between Tom and his older brother, she was reminded of how often she'd wished she had siblings growing up.

Three-year-old Sean was excited about the prospect of having a baby sister. The energetic toddler had his mother's eyes and his father's smile.

Callie dealt with children all the time, yet this was one of the few occasions when she wondered what it would be like to have a little one of her own—with her eyes and Tom's smile?

Whoa, where did that come from?

Her gaze flew to Tom. He was speaking to his nephew. He was surprisingly good with kids. No doubt he'd be every bit as good a dad as Striker clearly was.

She was learning more about him every moment. Tonight, she'd learned that he liked his steak rare with plenty of steak sauce. She noticed that he went out of his way to blend in, as if his injury didn't exist. She'd caught a wince when Sean had climbed onto his lap, but only because she'd been studying Tom's face at the time, noting how good he looked in profile.

Other than that one time when they'd had dinner at Jimmy Bob's Barbecue together, he never talked about what had happened to him or his physical condition. Never said *why me?*

Not that she expected anything less from a by-the-book Marine like him.

But she wondered what was going on beneath his tough exterior. Yes, he was a Marine, but he was also a man who had to have emotions—no matter how fiercely he denied them.

She had the feeling her wounded warrior was more comfortable fighting outer enemies than battling his own inner demons.

Her wounded warrior?

She'd do well to remember that Tom was his own man and his heart belonged to his family and the Marine Corps. Not to her.

The next week flew by for Callie. The last week of school each year always did.

Thursday was the final day for the kids—a play day. They began with a little goodbye circle, where Callie had her students pass around a teddy bear to indicate whose turn it was to say their goodbyes and talk about how they were going to spend their summers. Adam didn't even protest about not being first.

"We're going to Walt Disney World this summer," Anna said.

"We're going to the moon," Adam bragged when his turn came around.

The kids didn't dawdle inside, eager to participate in the picnic taking place on the playground. The smell of hot dogs on the grill led them outside, where stations manned by parent volunteers had been set up around the perimeter: a bubble station, a jump rope station, a face painting station. The older kids were signing up for relay races to take place after lunch.

But the star attraction was their special guest: Captain Tom Kozlowski. In dress blues.

On Monday, the kindergarten and first-grade students had voted for their special guest. Callie could still recall the stunned look on Tom's face when she'd told him the news.

"They what?" he said.

"They voted you as the person they'd most like to have attend their play day celebrations."

"Why?"

"Because they like you."

"I don't know those kids."

"You may not have spent much time at the school, but you still managed to make quite an impression."

"What does a special guest have to do?"

"Stand up and say a few words, eat your lunch with the kids and leave. Before you say no, let me add that it would only take about an hour of your time."

"How did you know I was going to say no?"

"I'm starting to learn to read that wrinkle you get in the middle of your forehead when you're about to say no."

"Marines do not wrinkle their foreheads."

"Not when they have their war faces on, no. But for their no-way-am-I-doing-that face, then yeah, they do. Or, at least, you do."

"You have a vivid imagination."

"That's very true, but it has nothing to do with this. Come on, it's only an hour. And it would mean so much to the kids, especially your buddy Quentin."

"I suppose I'd have to come in my uniform."

"I hadn't thought of that, but that would be cool. I mean, if you're okay with it."

"Why wouldn't I be?"

She just shrugged, not wanting to tell him that she didn't know if he'd worn the uniform at all since he'd been injured.

She still didn't know that, but here he was, sitting on a picnic bench in the middle of the playground. True, he did look a little like a fish out of water, with kids in shorts darting around him and parents chatting among themselves.

Even sitting down, Tom's posture was military erect, the hard lines of his body projecting leadership. The dark-blue of his jacket was immaculate, the brass buttons gleaming in the sunshine.

He looked incredibly good. Callie wasn't the only one who thought so. She'd caught several of the moms shooting him approving glances normally reserved for Brad Pitt.

The only one not impressed was Anna. "I voted for Happy the Clown," Anna told him.

"I voted for you," Quentin said. "The Captain is a Marine and he goes after bad guys…and girls," he added with a meaningful look at Anna.

"My blood sugar is off," Adam declared, a bit put out at being ignored.

"No, it's not," Anna retorted. "Ms. Murphy says your blood sugar is fine."

Adam waited until Anna had walked away before turning to Tom. "She's just mad because I'm a spy. Spies are even better than Marines."

"Unless you're a *Marine* spy," Quentin stated on Tom's behalf.

Adam looked suitably impressed.

Callie observed it all with amusement.

Once the boys had run off to the bubble station, Callie sat beside Tom. "So how are you holding up so far?

I see you've managed to avoid the nail polish and hair-braiding corner."

"Maybe I should have worn my cammies and cammy face paint as if this were a CAX—a combined arms exercise," he translated.

"You're in friendly territory here."

Her assurance didn't appear to help him relax.

A few minutes later, she had the kids settle down so that he could say a few words. "Now we'll have the kindergarten and first grade's special guest speak."

She nodded to Tom, who'd stood to address the students. "Behave and obey your teachers."

"And?" Callie prompted when he fell silent.

"And nothing."

"That's it?"

"Affirmative."

Adam's arm shot in the air, where he waved it wildly. He didn't wait for Callie to call on him before asking Tom, "What does that mean?"

"It means yes," Tom replied.

"Then why don't you just say yes?"

"It's a Marine thing," Quentin inserted. "Right, Captain?"

"Affirmative."

"We should have voted for Happy the Clown," Anna stated. "My sister in the fifth grade gets to listen to a firefighter."

Nobody insulted Tom's beloved Marine Corps, not even a crabby five-year-old.

"I'll bet neither Happy the Clown nor the fifth graders' firefighter has been in the jungle with wild monkeys throwing things at them."

"Happy has a monkey," Anna said.

"It's a toy monkey," Adam pointed out.

"Well, I'll tell you this much," Tom said, his voice filled with confidence and demanding their attention. "If you should ever find yourselves in a jungle with monkeys screeching all night and keeping you awake, do not throw anything at them."

"Because that wouldn't be polite," Anna said.

"Because they will throw it right back at you," Tom said.

The ice was broken and the kids started asking him all kinds of questions.

"Can girls be Marines, too?"

"How old are you?"

"Where's your wife?"

"Can I bring my cat if I join the Marines?"

Callie finally had to break things up, reminding everyone that the hot dogs were ready.

As the kids rushed to their eating area, supervised by parent volunteers, Callie sat beside Tom. "Thanks for being such a good sport about today. I owe you big time."

"Affirmative."

"Whatever you want. Takeout from Jimmy Bob's Barbecue? Homemade cookies? You name it."

"I'll have to give it some thought."

Callie certainly gave him some thought long after he'd left, his guest stint done.

The kids were still talking about him, as were the moms. "There's just something about a man in uniform," Adam's mom noted with a dreamy sigh.

"Especially *that* man. Talk about good-looking. And that scar on his cheek makes him look even more dangerous."

Even Paula made a few comments. "I'd say that Marine of yours got rave reviews for his appearance here today. I didn't think he'd really show up."

"Marines take their commitments very seriously," Callie replied. "Once he said yes, I knew he'd follow through."

"Did you have a hard time convincing him?"

"A little."

"What did you have to hold out as an incentive?" Paula wiggled her eyebrows.

"Nothing, and get that look off your face. And change the subject."

"Fine. Do you believe another year is almost done?"

"I know." Callie grinned. "We survived another year. Amazing, huh?"

"Totally."

Callie noted that Quentin was sitting with several other first graders, using colored chalk to draw on the sidewalk at the art station. His face was animated as he laughed with his friends.

Callie had to stay late that evening, putting in a four-teen-hour day. By the time she got home, she was too tired to do more than take a shower and roll into bed.

The next day was Callie's last day, and most of it was spent packing up the year's materials. After finishing her paperwork for the students' portfolios, she handed them over to Paula, their first-grade teacher.

Next, she removed everything from her bulletin boards. Their emptiness was a little bittersweet.

The kids in her class this year had made it a particularly satisfying group. Having finally completed everything on the official checklist, Callie turned it and her keys in to the principal before picking up her paycheck.

Another year was done.

Callie had no idea what next year's batch of kinder-gartners would be like.

She had no idea if her town house would be done on time.

And she had no idea if she would continue to have feelings for a Marine who made her laugh…and cry.

She had a sinking feeling that the answer to that last one might be a resounding yes.

A week went by and Tom couldn't believe that Callie made no effort to contact him, other than a friendly wave. When she'd invited him to her school, he'd at first thought it was a setup, that she wanted to spend more time with him.

Arrogant, he knew, given his less-than-perfect condition.

But then she'd thrown him by acting all…*normal.*

Not that she could try and seduce him with a bunch of rugrats running around. He got that.

He was also starting to get the idea that maybe he was the one all messed up. It certainly wasn't logical for him to be complaining because she'd stayed away.

She'd overheard him tell Kate to stop matchmaking, that if he wanted a woman, he'd get one.

But Tom wasn't interested in any other woman. Instead, he sat in his cabin, completing arm-curl reps with his weights and wondering where she was going every day. School was out now. So why did she still go out after completing her tai chi in the morning? Was she going to meet some guy?

What was she up to?

Why did he care? Maybe that was the more important question. Too bad he didn't know the answer to that one.

That night, his nightmare returned. The ambush played out in slow motion. He knew what was coming but couldn't prevent it. Couldn't wake up. The shouts. The gunfire. The sudden blast. A flash of red, blood, pain.

He jerked awake and sat up, dislodging Arf from the foot of the bed. It took Tom a second or two to realize that the rumble was thunder, not explosives.

That discovery didn't lessen the tight feeling in his chest. Needing fresh air, he headed outside on the front porch.

The storm blew in fast and fierce.

Arf stayed inside, safe and comfy on the bed.

Tom stayed outside, caught up in the elemental battle of nature. The wind was so intense it blew the sheets of rain sideways, wetting his bare feet. Not that he cared.

He did care when lightning flashed directly overhead, momentarily blinding him. A crack of thunder followed immediately.

Or was that more than just thunder?

Tom got up and looked out from his porch toward Callie's cabin. He swore under his breath when he realized that the tree shading the back of the cabin had cracked in two, one part falling on the roof.

He rushed out into the storm and toward her front door, cursing aloud as his leg slowed him more than he liked in the muddy ground.

The front door was unlocked. He didn't bother knocking. Instead, he opened it and yelled "Callie, are you okay?"

"Don't let the cat out!" she yelled back.

Muttering under his breath, he closed the door behind him.

"There's a tree in my bedroom," Callie told him from a few feet away. She was wearing a San Antonio Spurs nightshirt. "Actually, it's just a branch. It broke the window and there's glass everywhere. You have bare feet. You better not go in there." She pointed her flashlight from his feet up to his face.

"What is it with you teachers that you have to boss people around?"

"What is it with you Marines that you object to being bossed around?"

"It's my job."

"Mine, too."

"You obviously can't stay here tonight. You better come over to my place."

"No way."

Her refusal caught him by surprise.

"You just said that there's a tree in your bedroom," he pointed out.

"A branch," she corrected him. "And a broken window. And maybe a hole in the roof. Some rain damage. But that's okay."

"No, it's not. You're coming to my place," he stated emphatically.

"No, I'm not," she stated just as emphatically.

"Why not?"

"Because I'm not having you accuse me later of setting this up as some kind of matchmaking scam. I don't want you throwing that in my face again."

"Callie, while I think you probably could move mountains, even you can't direct lightning strikes. Come on."

She shook her head.

"Look, you have my word as a Captain of the United States Marine Corps that I won't accuse you of anything."

She still remained silent.

Tom decided it was time to haul out the big guns. "Bob can come along, too."

Chapter Nine

The pounding woke him up the next morning. At first, Tom thought it was men making repairs to the damage caused by the storm. Then he realized that the sound was coming from his front door.

Whoever it was wasn't going away.

Yanking on a pair of workout pants, Tom barely avoided tripping over a still-sleeping Arf as he opened his bedroom door and came face-to-face with Callie. Even in his grouchy mood, he noticed that she looked incredibly good wearing his shirt and a pair of socks.

"There's someone at your door," she told him.

"No kidding."

"Thomas!" a woman outside shouted.

He groaned. "It's my grandmother."

"Wait. Don't open the door yet," Callie said, but it was too late.

His grandmother Wanda Kozlowski stood on the front porch. Despite barely reaching five feet, she had a huge personality and a smile that could light up her whole face. She was not smiling at the moment, though. The woman standing beside her was equally petite and equally larger than life personalitywise.

"What is going on in here?" Tex demanded.

"It's *your* grandmother, too," Tom told Callie, who had a definite deer-caught-in-headlights thing going on.

"You are living with a woman?" Wanda's voice reflected her disapproval. "Without marriage?"

"You no-good son-of-a-sea dog!" Tex exclaimed in outrage.

Wanda turned on Tex. "My Thomas is the son of a Marine, and who are you to insult my grandson so?"

"I'm Callie's grandmother."

"You are this hussy's grandmother? She clearly took advantage of my injured grandson."

"Are you loco?"

"No, I am Wanda."

"You're crazier than a lizard with sunstroke if you think my granddaughter had anything to do with this situation. She's a kindergarten teacher." Tex gave Tom the evil eye. "And she better still be a virgin or you'll be staring down the wrong end of a shotgun, mister high-and-mighty Marine."

"Gran!" Callie looked ready to sink through the floor.

"It's *Captain* high-and-mighty Marine," Tom drawled.

Callie smacked his bare shoulder. "This is no time for humor."

"So you think this is funny, do you?" Tex moved forward, ready to give him the full force of her anger.

She was stopped in her tracks by Wanda, who

stepped in front of her and warned her, "Do not even think about threatening my poor Thomas. He was injured fighting for his country, for *your* freedom. And this is how you repay him?"

"That doesn't give him the right to seduce my granddaughter," Tex stated.

Wanda sniffed. "She doesn't appear to mind wearing his shirt, so if there is any seducing going on, it is by her. Maybe she's a gold digger after his money."

"That's enough, Busha...." Tom warned.

"I thought you said your name was Wanda," Tex noted suspiciously.

"It is. Wanda Kozlowski. *Busha* is the Polish word for grandmother."

"Polish, huh? I thought you had a funny accent," Tex said.

"Me?" Wanda raised an eyebrow. "I speak perfect English. You are the one who speaks strangely."

Tex narrowed her eyes at her. "You're in Texas now. You better get used to it."

"Get used to a woman accusing my Thomas of unspeakable misdeeds?" Wanda countered. "I think not."

"No unspeakable misdeeds took place here," Tom said. "Tell them, Callie."

"No unspeakable misdeeds took place here," she repeated dutifully. "Um, I'll just go get dressed...."

"And miss the rest of the show?" Tom said.

She smacked him again.

"You're not going anywhere until you tell me what you're doing wearing his shirt in his cabin," Tex stated.

"Yes, this I would like to know also," Wanda said.

"There was a big storm in the middle of the night and it damaged the roof of the cabin next door where I was staying," Callie explained. "Lightning hit a tree right behind the cabin and the wind blew part of the roof right off."

"The storm also blew your clothes off?" Wanda asked.

Callie blushed. "No, of course not. But the rain poured into the closet where I stored my clothes. I put them in the dryer first thing this morning. Tom lent me this shirt last night to sleep in and to wear until my things are dry."

"He couldn't lend you anything that would cover you up more?" Tex demanded.

"I'm so much shorter than he is that nothing else fit," Callie said.

"Where did you sleep?"

"In the guest room." Callie pointed to the spare room.

"What is that strange noise?" Wanda asked.

"That's Arf," Tom said. "My dog."

The animal peered at them from behind the bedroom door.

"You did not tell me you had a poodle, Thomas."

"He's not a poodle," Tom protested.

"Looks like a poodle to me," Tex agreed. "What's he doing? Sounds like he's whimpering."

"He's barking," Tom stated. "Quietly."

Tex wasn't buying that for one minute. "Sounds more like whimpering to me. A real girlie poodle dog, huh?"

Tom heard what he thought was a growl from Arf at this insult, but the noise turned out to be Bob purring as he wound himself around Callie's bare ankles.

"Do not insult my grandson's dog. At least he's not obese like that animal." Wanda pointed to Bob.

Knowing that Callie was liable to go ballistic over an insult aimed at her pet, Tom hurriedly spoke up. "Okay, ladies, let's call a truce, shall we?"

"That'll happen when a rooster lays an egg," Tex stated.

"What kind of silly talk is that?" Wanda demanded. "Everyone knows that roosters do not lay eggs."

"It's a Texas saying."

"Polish sayings are much better. God grant me a sword and no use for it. Now that is a worthy saying."

"Are you threatening my granddaughter with a sword?" Tex demanded. "Because you don't want to be messin' with Texas or with Tex Murphy."

Wanda frowned. "Who is Tex Murphy?"

Tex proudly jabbed her thumb at her chest. "I am."

"That is a man's name—"

"Ladies," Tom quickly interrupted. "If I could have your attention, please?"

"See how polite he is?" Wanda bragged. "My grandson knows his manners."

"Not if he's fixin' to seduce my granddaughter, he doesn't."

"He is handsome and rich. And Polish. Girls chase after him all the time."

"He's just a jarhead to me."

"There is nothing wrong with his head!" Wanda said indignantly.

"*Jarhead* is just a nickname for a Marine," Tom assured his grandmother.

"More of this strange Texas language?" Wanda asked.

"No, actually, we can't blame that one on Texas," Tom said.

"I would have thought you'd know about jarheads, what with you havin' so many of them in your family." Tex directed the challenge to Wanda.

"What are you two doing here so early in the morning?" Tom quickly inserted.

Wanda frowned. "It's almost eight-thirty. That's not early."

"I came to check up on my granddaughter," Tex said, "and it's clearly a good thing that I did."

"I don't need checking up on," Callie protested.

Tex pointed a finger at Tom. "He's AWOL."

"He is not!" Callie immediately defended him. "He's on a medical leave of absence."

"AWOL," Tex repeated. "A wolf on the loose."

"My Thomas is not a wolf!" Wanda was outraged.

"Well, my Callie is not a hussy!" Tex was equally affronted.

"Ladies, ladies." Tom held out his arms as if to keep them apart. "This isn't getting us anywhere."

"Anywhere? Why? Where were you fixin' on goin'?" Tex demanded. "Back into that bedroom of yours to besmirch my granddaughter's reputation?"

Tom lifted an eyebrow. "Besmirch?"

Tex narrowed her eyes at him. "Are you makin' fun of my vocabulary?"

"I wouldn't dream of it."

"I would," Wanda said.

"How did you get out here, Busha?" Tom asked belatedly.

"Kate had a ranch hand drop me off."

A second later, his cellphone rang. It was Kate. "Your Busha is on her way out there."

"Too late, she's already here. I'll call you back later." He returned his attention to the two grandmothers, standing like opposing gunslingers at high noon. "So where were we, ladies?"

"I need to speak to my granddaughter in private," Tex stated.

The moment the two women closed the door on the

spare bedroom, Wanda turned to Tom. "Aren't you going to give your Busha a hug?"

"Sure." He moved forward. It never ceased to amaze him that, despite her petite stature, she really was a powerhouse, even at her age. And she had the bluest eyes. They could look right through you. They were doing that as he released her.

"So what is going on here, Thomas?"

"Nothing. Didn't you hear the storm last night?"

"I heard nothing. But then I sleep soundly."

"I'll bet Kate heard the storm."

"I do not want to talk about the storm. I want to talk about that girl."

"Tex is Striker's executive assistant. Callie is her granddaughter."

"I gathered that much. What is this Callie to you?"

"Nothing."

"There was chemistry going on here." Wanda shook her finger at him. "Do not think that I didn't notice that."

"You're imagining things."

"Not true."

"Nice T-shirt," Tom commented, pointing to the No One Is Ever Old Enough to Know Better line. His grandmother always was one for bright colors and humorous sayings.

"Yes, it is, but do not try to distract me. Do not think you can pull the wool over my eyes."

"I'd never—"

"Yes, you would." She studied him for a moment before relenting. "Fine. I'll let you have your secrets for now. We will talk again soon—when we have more privacy," she added as Tex stepped out of the spare bedroom.

"I'm getting Callie's clothes from the dryer," Tex stated as if daring either of them to stop her.

"It's just off the kitchen," Tom told her.

Tex was on her way back with an armful of clothes when Striker appeared at the still-open front door.

"You just missed the showdown," Tom told him.

"Tex called me and said the cabin was damaged in that storm last night."

"You can't tell from the front," Tex said. "But when I looked out the spare bedroom window, I saw the huge tree branch."

"I'll go check it out," Striker said.

It took the better part of an hour to get rid of everyone. Striker left with Wanda, promising to get repairs done as quickly as possible.

Tex left under her own steam, which was practically pouring out of her ears when Callie refused to go with her. "You could sleep on the couch at my place."

"Gran, you're allergic to cats."

"You could leave Bob here."

"It will only be for a short time. Just the weekend. You heard Striker say that all the bedrooms up at the ranch house are filled with his grandmother and his parents visiting."

"Do not make me come after you," Tex warned Tom with a steely-eyed look.

"Gran…" Callie warned her. She put an arm around her grandmother's shoulders and guided her out the door. "…I'll see you later this afternoon—at the party," she added in a whisper in case Striker hadn't left yet. "Don't worry about a thing. I'm perfectly safe here."

Once she'd finally gone, Tom turned to Callie. Both of them had managed to put clothes on. She was wearing jeans and a white shirt. Her hair was loose around her shoulders.

"Well, that's something else we have in common," Callie noted with a grin. "Strong-willed grandmothers."

"With accents," Tom said.

"And pride in their heritage."

"A granny showdown at the OK Corral."

Callie laughed. "It did sort of feel that way, didn't it?"

"No *sort of* about it. I expected Tex to haul out her six-shooter any minute."

"My grandmother is not a violent person."

"Of course she's not," Tom mocked her. "That comment she made before leaving about cutting off certain parts of my body should I ever attempt to deflower you was just a joke, no doubt."

"Oh no, I'm sure she was serious about that."

Tom winced. "Gee, thanks."

"She has strong opinions about certain things."

"No kidding."

"Your grandmother seemed the same way."

"What way is that? Crazed?"

"No. Old-fashioned. She was certainly passionate in her defense of you."

"The Poles are a passionate people."

"So are Texans."

"That's becoming clear to me."

"Seems like mixing the two could end up with explosive results." She winced after realizing her choice of words wasn't the best to use in front of a man who'd been injured in an explosion. "Sorry, I meant—"

"I know what you meant. And I agree. Two intense personalities like that would be like mixing oil and water."

"Not that I'm as intense as my grandmother is."

"You do have red hair."

She shoved the loose strands away from her face. "So what? That means that I automatically have a volatile personality? That is such a cliché!"

"So is thinking that all rich people are arrogant."

His words clearly caught her by surprise. "I have my reasons."

"Which are?"

"Ones I don't care to talk about at the moment. How about I cook us some breakfast instead?"

As she got busy in the kitchen, Tom was left wondering what she was hiding. Had some rich guy done her wrong? Her grandmother claimed that Callie was still a virgin, but that didn't mean it was true. Had Callie had her heart broken and her virginity stolen by some wealthy scumbag?

Tom clenched his hands into fists. He wanted to punch the guy's lights out.

A strong reaction for a man who claimed nothing was going on between Callie and him.

"Okay, everyone," Kate told the group gathered in the great room at the ranch. "Be quiet. I think they're coming now."

"Surprise!!" everyone yelled a second later.

The only one surprised was Stan Kozlowski, Striker and Tom's dad.

"Wrong Kozlowski," Striker's mom noted with a grin.

"What are you doing outside? Everyone is supposed to stay inside until they come. Never mind." Kate turned to the rest of the group. "Clearly, I need a spotter to check out who's coming in the front door. Tony—"

Kate pointed to the longtime ranch foreman "—stand by the door and look for Striker and Wanda to return from the Alamo."

Callie was amazed at Kate's energy in getting all this arranged. The room was filled with family—Kate's and Striker's—and longtime friends. "That was a clever idea to have Wanda insist that Striker take her on a tour of the Alamo today," Callie congratulated her.

"It was Tom's idea actually."

"Really?" Callie looked across the room, where Tom was speaking to his parents.

She could definitely see the resemblance in the way both Tom and his dad carried themselves. She hadn't had a chance to speak to his parents yet, since Tex had kept Callie pretty close to her side since arriving at the ranch.

"Yes. I couldn't have done this without his help, despite his protests that he wanted nothing to do with it," Kate said. "Oh, here comes Tony."

"Striker has just pulled up," Tony announced.

"Okay, everyone." Kate waved her hands. "Places."

"I'm starving," Striker could be heard saying out in the foyer.

"I'll make you some of my special *kolachkis*," Wanda promised him.

Striker walked into the room, where everyone once again yelled "Surprise!"

Callie couldn't tell if Striker was really surprised or not, but he did put on a good show for the crowd. His young son, Sean, shrieked louder than anyone, clearly enjoying the party atmosphere.

"Justice!" Striker seemed genuinely pleased and amazed to see his old friend. "I didn't know you'd be here. I didn't know anyone would be here," he quickly added when Kate shot him a look.

Justice, a man of apparently few words, just thumped Striker on the back in some sort of male bonding ritual.

"Everybody…" Striker raised his voice to get their attention. "…this is Justice Wilder, an old Force Recon buddy of mine."

"Watch who you're calling old," Justice growled.

A clearly unrepentant Striker just grinned. "And his wife, Kelly."

"And our little girl, Natalie," a smiling Kelly added.

Tom noticed the way Callie seemed to keep to the outer edges of the gathering, as if hesitant to join in. That surprised him. He'd always thought of her as a confident woman in the thick of things.

Aside from Kate's parents, who radiated upper-crust class and old-time money, most of the people in this room were not wealthy, so that couldn't be what was keeping her back.

When Tom saw her stroll out onto the poolside patio, he followed her.

"Having a good time?" he asked.

She appeared startled. "I didn't see you there."

"You didn't answer my question."

"Sure, I'm having a good time. Who wouldn't? The food is delicious."

"The ribs aren't as good as Jimmy Bob's," Tom noted with a slow smile.

Callie smiled back. "No, they aren't. But they're still pretty good."

Noticing her looking at the pool, he said, "Thinking of taking another swim?"

"No way. I didn't bring my swimsuit."

"Has your grandmother recovered yet from the fact that we're living together?"

"Do not say anything to set her off again," Callie warned him.

"*Moi?*" Tom placed his hand on his chest and gave her a wounded look. "As if I would do such a thing."

"Yes, you. Making fun of her that way."

"What way?"

"Besmirched."

He grinned. "You have to admit, it's not a word you hear much anymore."

"Doesn't mean that there isn't plenty of besmirching going on behind closed doors."

Her gaze got tangled up in his. The image of him with her behind closed doors was enough to get Tom's body all riled up. She was wearing a demure floral sundress with her hair pinned on top of her head. The sweet innocence of her attire only made him want her more.

"Tom, do you have a minute?" Justice called out.

Tom yanked his attention away from Callie, the Marine rather than the man regaining control.

"Affirmative," Tom replied.

"I'd better get back inside," Callie murmured, leaving the two men alone.

"So how's the recovery going?" Justice asked.

"Fine."

"Understood. That's what I said when I didn't want to talk about my condition. I don't know if Striker told you my story."

Tom knew that Justice had stayed at Striker's beach house after being injured. Since Justice was Striker's best friend and a fellow Marine, Tom had known him, too—although not as well as Striker did.

"He told me that your shoulder was injured," Tom replied.

"Not in the line of fire. When I was off duty. There

was a car crash and I...well, the details aren't important."

"Yes, they are," his wife interjected as she joined them. "He saved a child's life."

"At the expense of my future as a Marine." Justice's words were clipped. "My injury prevented me from returning to Force Recon."

"What did you do?" Tom asked.

"Almost bit my head off every chance he got," Kelly replied.

"She's a physical therapist," Justice said. He paused to put his arm around his wife. "I finally realized that someone up there had bigger plans for me. And I'm not talking about a plan from someone at the Pentagon."

Tom nodded. "Understood."

"There were still ways that I could contribute to my fellow Marines. I teach new groups of Force Recon wannabes. See if they have what it takes." Justice paused to give Tom a chance to reply. When he didn't, Justice continued on. "All I'm saying is that, just like in war planning, you have to be open to new options because the mission is changing all the time. Conditions change. But the goal remains the same. Understood?"

Tom nodded. But something deep inside of him rebelled at the idea that he'd never return to active duty. He liked being in the thick of things. He wasn't one to sit around and twiddle his thumbs.

Not that what Justice was doing fell under that category.

But Tom wasn't ready to accept anything less than returning to 100 percent. Which was why he continued his physical therapy with steadfast determination, always doing more than what was asked of him.

Because that's what a Marine did.

They sucked it up and managed.

Failure was not an option.

Tom had become an expert at slamming the hatch on any negative thoughts. Except for the nightmares that sometimes slipped past his defenses.

Like last night, when that storm had hit.

Callie watched Tom speaking with Justice and wondered what the two men were talking about that gave them both such stern faces.

"Did I ever apologize to you?" Kate said.

Guilty of being caught staring at Tom, Callie turned to face her. "Apologize for what?"

"For getting hormonal that evening you came over for dinner."

"No apology is necessary."

"Did Tom apologize for what he said that day?"

Callie nodded.

"I thought he would. He's really a good guy, you know. He has that big, strong, tough exterior, which I think maybe he has to project even more since he was in that ambush. We almost lost him, you know. He almost died."

Callie rubbed her hands up her arms as a cold shiver ran through her.

"It changed him," Kate noted. "How could it not? Tom had already donated a sizable amount of money to the Fallen Patriots Fund. While he was recovering, he donated even more of his inheritance. Claimed he was tired of females chasing after him for his money—as if that were the only reason women noticed him. No way. I tried to tell him that, but he wasn't in any mood to listen to his sister-in-law's opinion of things, you know what I mean?"

Callie nodded.

Kate was called away by another guest, but she was replaced by Wanda. Despite the older woman's initial misgivings about her, she appeared to have come around and gave Callie a friendly smile.

"I hope you are not angry that I thought you had seduced my Thomas."

"No."

"Or that I called your cat fat."

"That was harder to forgive," Callie noted with a grin.

"Ah, you have a sense of humor." Wanda patted Callie's arm. "This is a good thing. You will need it to deal with Thomas."

"I've discovered that." She belatedly realized that her words made it sound like there was more to their relationship than there actually was. "We're just friends, though."

Wanda nodded her approval. "Which is a good thing. It is good to be friends with the person you love."

"No, no, you've got it all wrong."

"Ah, so you are not yet ready to accept it." Her blue eyes seemed so wise as she gently touched Callie's cheek. "That's all right. Sometimes it takes a little more time. That's how it was for Chloe. She is Thomas's twin brother's wife. She was also my next-door neighbor, you know."

"No, I didn't know that." She did know that Wanda fancied herself a matchmaker for her grandsons. Tom had filled her in earlier. Callie felt she had to make things clear here. "Look, Tom bluntly told Kate that he didn't want her matchmaking. That if he wanted a woman, he'd go out and get one."

"But he hasn't done that. Instead, he's living with you."

"Actually, I'm living with him. And it's only temporary. Just until the repairs can be made on the other cabin."

"I have seen the way he looks at you. And the way you look at him."

Callie didn't know what to say about that, so she pointed to the buffet table, trying to distract Wanda with food. "Have you tried the sour mango coleslaw?"

"I put that out for Striker as a reminder of our first date," Kate declared as she meandered by.

"I am not a sour mango coleslaw kind of guy," Striker immediately stated. "No way that skunk is gonna mate."

Wanda shook her head. "I can't get used to all these crazy sayings."

"You always told us plenty of Polish sayings when we were growing up," Striker reminded his grandmother.

"Of course. You come from a proud heritage. And Polish sayings are good. Talking about skunks having sex—" Wanda waved her hands as if she could make the words disappear "—I don't see the appeal there."

Striker grimaced. "I can't get used to my Busha talking about sex."

"Hasn't your father told you that I'm doing more than talking about it?" Wanda retorted.

Striker looked like he'd swallowed an armadillo.

He sputtered and choked, forcing Tom to come in from the patio and thump him on the back.

Striker glared at him. "You didn't have to hit me that hard."

Tom grinned. "Sure I did. I hear that as you get older, you have these kinds of episodes."

"Your Busha just told Striker something that startled him," Kate replied.

"What did you say, Busha?" Tom asked.

"No, don't repeat it," Striker ordered her.

Wanda waved a reprimanding finger at him. "You are like your father and your brothers. They all have hissy fits when I mention sex. I thought you would have heard by now about my significant other, Patrick O'Hara."

"Significant other?" Striker repeated in a strangled voice.

"Well, *boyfriend* sounds too silly when you reach my age," Wanda said.

"So the two of you are…dating?" Tom asked.

Wanda laughed, a supersized sound. "We are doing more than dating."

"Too much information!" Striker held out his hands as if he could put the words back into Wanda's mouth.

Tom had another complaint. "In that case, Busha, you had no excuse for reprimanding me when you thought Callie and I were living together."

"Because you are young. You should be married."

"So should you," Tom retorted.

Wanda smiled. "That's what Patrick said when he asked me."

"He asked you to marry him?" The question came from Tom.

Wanda nodded. "I said I would think about it while I was here. He is going to come down to visit me next week."

"What does Dad have to say about all this?"

Wanda laughed again. "Your father says nothing. That is how he is. Your mother is pleased for me, though."

As Callie watched the interaction between the Kozlowskis, she was once again struck by the love they had for one another. Despite the differences, despite the distance, there was a genuine affection among the family members that was quite endearing to someone who'd grown up without siblings or an extended family.

A few minutes later, Callie spoke to Tex in a quiet corner. "Wanda is thinking of getting married. Her husband passed away some time ago. Did you ever consider getting married again?"

Tex shook her head. "I like my independence."

"What about Dad? Do you know if he ever considered marrying again?"

"Your mother was the love of his life. He knew that and wouldn't settle for anything less."

"Do you really think there's only one person meant for you?"

"There's only one love of your life, one soul mate."

Callie tried not to stare at Tom as she asked the question burning in her mind. "How do you know which one is *the* one?"

"You just do."

"So you knew once you met Grandfather that he was the one?"

"Fat chance. I wasn't sure at all. Not at first. But he sure did grow on me mighty fast. Why are you askin' me these questions now? You're not fixin' to get hitched, are you?"

"It was just because of what Wanda said about her getting married."

"I haven't forgotten she called you a hussy. You're my pride and joy. I fight to protect my family."

"I know you do." Callie gave her grandmother a hug. "But there's no need. Tom is as honorable as his brother, and you think the world of Striker, I know you do."

"Don't let him hear you sayin' that," Tex muttered.

"Saying what?" Striker demanded.

"I swear, you have ears in the back of your head."

Striker just grinned. "Like I told my wife, it's hard to get anything past a former Force Recon Marine."

"Who still doesn't know how to use the fax machine," Tex added.

"I delegate certain responsibilities to other members of the mission team."

"He's talking about me," Tex told Callie before returning her attention to Striker. "Do I have your word that my granddaughter's reputation will be safe with your brother?"

"That's a question you should be asking me," Tom said as he joined them. "Not my brother."

"Fine." Tex turned to face Tom. "I'm askin' you then."

"Yes, you have my word," he immediately replied.

"As a Marine?"

Tom nodded. "As a Marine."

"Good. I'm glad to hear that."

"I'm not!" Callie said.

At the startled looks of those around her, Callie realized that could be taken the wrong way. "I didn't mean that I wanted him to…uh, what I did mean is that I am an adult, Gran. What I do is my business."

As Callie's eyes met Tom's, she wondered if soul mates were a figment of someone's imagination or if she was gazing at the one man who was meant for her.

Chapter Ten

Saturday. Tom glanced down at his watch. Thirty-four hours and counting with Callie as his roomie.

Mission goal: To stay calm. Detached. In control.

Mission success: Extremely uncertain.

Situation update: Watching Callie play solitaire on her laptop made him want to kiss her.

Watching her get up and boil water for her tea made him want to kiss her.

Watching her nibble on a cookie made him want to take her to bed and have her nibble on him.

The woman was driving him crazy and she wasn't even trying, which made Tom wonder what it would be like if she really did try to seduce him.

All kinds of possible scenarios filled his head—most of them more suitable to an adults-only cable channel than to an officer of the United States Marine Corps who'd sworn on his honor that Callie's virtue would be safe with him.

Didn't mean a guy couldn't dream, though.

As long as that's all he did.

Callie was strictly hands-off. Didn't matter that he could smell her strawberry soap in the bathroom. Didn't matter that she looked adorable first thing in the morning.

She was off-limits.

She deserved more than he could give her.

His attention strayed from Callie to the exercise equipment in the corner of the cabin. She hadn't commented on it, for which he was grateful. He'd completed his early morning workout while she'd been doing her tai chi outside.

Tom was determined to keep his physical condition as prime as possible. In addition to his physical therapy, he'd become an expert at the so-called joys of weight lifting, both here at the cabin and at the military hospital.

After he'd completed his workouts at the hospital, he spent hours talking to other Marines injured far worse than he'd been, keeping their spirits up, monitoring their progress, motivating them to keep trying.

Which sometimes made him feel like a total fraud, given the fact that deep inside he was floundering.

Not that he had allowed anyone to see that.

But then Tom didn't work with the injured Marines in order to make *himself* feel any better. He did it because he was an officer, and even if they weren't in his command, they were Marines in need.

And the Marine Corps' code of duty was clear. No man was left behind. *No one.*

Marines never abandon their wounded. And not just on the battlefield but afterward, as well. Visiting burn victims and trying to cheer them up with some of the bawdier tall tales he'd heard from his Texas granddad was the least Tom could do.

"I don't believe it," Callie said.

At first, Tom thought she was talking about him doing more to help others.

"I don't believe how well Bob and Arf are getting along."

Callie had tried to keep her cat in the spare room with her, but that hadn't lasted long. Bob had slipped past her and come face-to-face with Arf in the living room last night. A sleeping Arf.

After sniffing the dog, Bob had calmly flopped down beside the aforementioned canine and started washing himself.

"I thought they'd fight like cats and dogs," Tom said.

"Me, too. Guess we shouldn't jump to conclusions like that."

"It was a conclusion based on past behavior," Tom pointed out.

"Things change."

"Maybe that lightning strike gave Bob a personality change."

The cat, which was presently curled up on an oval rug in front of the fireplace, lifted his head and gave Tom a dirty look.

"That animal of yours is downright eerie," Tom declared. "It's like he knows what I'm saying."

"He's very smart," Callie agreed. "I got him as a stray kitten from a local animal shelter. He's grown some since then."

"That's an understatement," Tom drawled.

Another dirty look from Bob was a clear warning not to say anything further about his weight.

Callie gathered up her hair in a ponytail before saying, "I think I'll go wash my car."

Tom held out a good fifteen minutes before giving in to temptation and going outside to sit on the front porch and watch her. Supposedly, he was doing arm curls with weights, but his attention remained focused on Callie.

The sudden press of a cold, wet nose on his bare feet reminded him that Arf had come outside with him. Looking down, he saw that his faithful buddy had fallen asleep. Surprise, surprise. A sudden twitch of the dog's leg indicated that Arf was dreaming.

What did dogs dream about?

What did Callie dream about?

Marriage and kids? Probably. She was that kind of woman. The kind you got serious about, not the kind you fooled around with.

True, he'd mistaken her profession that first night, but he hadn't really been in his right mind at that time. Not that he was all that sure he was in his right mind now, either.

Otherwise, he'd be off somewhere doing something else instead of sitting here admiring the way Callie looked wearing denim cutoffs and a light blue tank top that showed her creamy skin as she leaned across the car's hood to wipe it down.

The drone of insects provided accompaniment to the music she was listening to. He didn't recognize the song. Of course, he could barely hear it, not because his hearing was bad but because she had the volume politely low.

That's what was aggravating him. She was being really polite. Not that she'd been rude before. But she'd just done her thing and to heck with him.

Now it was as if she was trying to minimize her intrusion in his world, which, of course, was impossible to do.

The other night, his heart had stopped during the storm when that tree had been hit by lightning and he'd been afraid for her safety.

Spending so much time with her over the past thirty-four hours and counting had only made him want her more.

Maybe he was "in want" with her. Not "in need" because that would mean he was vulnerable. And certainly not "in love" because that would be just plain stupid.

The bottom line here was that, despite the many hours of rehab he'd put in, his entire future still remained very much up in the air.

No way could he be in love with Callie given that reality.

"In want" sounded better to him.

More manageable.

Because that's what Marines did. They sucked it up and they managed.

Whatever the situation.

No excuses.

No exceptions.

Callie was aware that Tom was sitting on his front porch while she washed the car. He was wearing aviator-style sunglasses, so she couldn't tell if he was actually looking at her or not. She could tell that the muscles of his arm rippled as he completed each arm curl.

She knew firsthand how hard those arms were. How protective. How seductive.

He was wearing shorts and the torn-sleeve T-shirt that she admired so much. She doubted that had played any part in him selecting his attire, however.

Last night, he'd looked polished and powerful. Today, he looked ruggedly sexy but still powerful.

Callie couldn't help thinking about what Kate had told her about Tom last night: that he'd donated the majority of his inheritance to charity. That could well mean that he no longer qualified as being rich.

So if that hurdle was overcome, now what was keeping her from falling for him? Her own sense of self-preservation?

Had Paula been right when she'd said that Callie didn't want to risk falling for Tom because she didn't want to risk having her heart broken by him?

He'd come out and told her point-blank that he wasn't interested in starting anything with her. And then he'd just as bluntly told his sister-in-law to stop throwing him and Callie together.

Still, there was this chemistry between them. This morning, when she was playing solitaire on her laptop, she could feel his eyes on her. His gaze had been as seductive as a caress.

Surely she hadn't imagined the hungry passion she'd seen in his eyes?

No one else in his family had eyes like his. His mom had shared that info with her for some reason last night. Angela Kozlowski had pretty green eyes. Striker's eyes were okay. But there was just something about Tom's eyes that totally got to Callie.

So what was she afraid of? Was she scared that if she let Tom get too close he'd discover that she wasn't really the woman he thought she was?

She was an impostor, pretending to be confident and in control when there were plenty of times she felt unsure and isolated deep inside.

Put her in a classroom in front of a group of kids and she could rule the world.

But in a situation where she felt like a fish out of water, those old high-school feelings of being the social misfit came rushing right back.

Luckily, the entire Kozlowski family had gone out of their way to make her feel as if she were one of them at Striker's surprise party last night.

Callie dropped her sponge in the bucket of soapy water as she continued trying to figure things out. Was Paula right? Had Callie's faith in happy endings died with her mother? Should she follow her friend's advice and have faith that things could work out?

The questions kept tumbling around inside her head, but the answers refused to come.

Callie had just finished rinsing off her car with the garden hose when Tom suddenly appeared at her side and handed her a glass of lemonade.

"Thanks." She took a sip.

While she'd been laboring away, some of her hair had escaped the confines of her ponytail.

Tom reached out and brushed the dampened strands away from her eyes, tucking them behind her ear.

His touch was gentle.

Her reaction was powerful.

He'd removed his sunglasses so she could see his eyes.

But before she could try to decipher what she saw there, he startled her by asking, "Why have you got a thing against rich guys?"

She took a step back. "There are too many reasons to get into."

"So you admit it?"

Callie nodded.

"I wasn't born rich, or even raised that way, you know," he said.

She nodded again. "I know."

Tom didn't push her. He shouldn't even care that she had issues the size of Texas.

But he did.

And that was a problem.

Because caring about her conflicted with his duty to keep his distance from her.

Not that he was about to put his hands up and surrender to her wiles. He was a fighter. He didn't give in and he didn't give up.

He'd had another nightmare last night. It had been particularly vivid. Unlike the others, it had focused on his time in the hospital, where he'd regained consciousness in a white bed. Tubes were connected to every part of him. His body burned as if someone had rammed him through a concrete mixer. At the complete mercy of others. Unable to do anything for himself.

Tom broke into a cold sweat at the memory, his mind still battling the images he'd worked so hard to forget.

Wheeling around, he walked away, willing himself not to look back at Callie.

His mission was clear: regain his strength and mobility, or die trying.

"Are you angry with me?" Callie voiced the question to Tom over the spaghetti dinner she'd prepared for them later that night. "Because you've been acting strangely ever since you gave me that lemonade this afternoon."

"Define *strangely*."

"Quiet."

"A perfectly normal state."

She couldn't challenge him on that. True, Tom never had been the chatty sort. But he usually spoke his mind and seemed to take pleasure in teasing her, or pushing her buttons, as he called it.

But after he'd surprised her by asking her why she had a thing against rich guys that afternoon, he'd seemed to retreat as if he regretted showing any curiosity about her.

But his long, silent glances in her direction spoke volumes. At least, they did to her.

Not that he did it in an obvious way. But she'd caught him watching her in that special way that made her heart do excited flip-flops.

A perfectly normal state, to use Tom's words. He had a way of getting to her without saying a word. She derived pleasure from merely watching him devour the meal she'd made. But Callie knew she really had it bad when she realized that she even liked the way he held his fork.

"Do you want to watch a DVD?" he asked her after they'd cleared up the dishes.

They'd worked side by side in the kitchen with a camaraderie that she hadn't expected. Oh, the sexual tension was still there. But so was the normalcy of washing dishes, of drying them and putting them away, of being part of a team.

He'd asked her a question. What had he said again? DVD. Right. "Sure. What did you have in mind?"

"How about *Star Wars,* since it played such an important role in our career choices?"

She was pleased that he'd remembered their earlier conversation about that. It seemed like that had happened so long ago.

And so they sat side by side on the couch, Callie

curled up with her feet tucked under her. The popcorn bowl started out between them, but somehow it ended up on her lap.

At one point, Tom's fingers brushed her bare thighs just below her cutoffs as he reached for another handful of popcorn.

Joyful awareness shot through her like that lightning bolt the other night. Her eyes flew to his. He kept his gaze on the TV, so she couldn't read his expression.

Their close proximity was definitely making the attraction more difficult to resist. Sitting beside him like this felt so good. So right. And not just because he was sexy, but because he made her laugh and made her think.

They'd just finished a lively discussion of how good a Marine Han Solo would have made when Tom noted, "I come from a family of overachievers."

"I noticed that," she said.

"I'm surprised we never ran into each other that summer I spent with my grandfather."

"We kind of crossed paths once. A long time ago. At a square dance." The memory had been slow in coming back to her, but it was clear now.

"Really? Were you that pretty girl in the blue dress at the square dance?"

"No."

"Are you sure?"

"Positive. I wasn't pretty."

"I find that hard to believe."

"It's the truth. I was…different then."

"What do you mean?"

This was the moment of truth. One of those forks in the road where you can choose the safe route or take a risk and let someone see the truth.

Callie swallowed the nervous knot in her throat and turned away from the smooth road she'd always taken in the past and instead picked the bumpy one, filled with possibilities.

She took a deep breath before speaking. "I was a dork in school, the one the other kids picked on. I mean, I was a *real* geek. Awkward and shy. My hair was more orange than red and I was pale, without a trace of a tan. Everybody made fun of me." She took another gulp of air. "When I went to a ritzy private school the teasing got even worse. I was attending on a scholarship. I totally didn't fit in with the wealthy students. One day, a bunch of girls decided that it would be fun to lock me in a tiny storage closet in the school's basement. I was in there for hours. They'd lured me down by saying that they felt guilty for being so mean to me before and that they wanted to make up for it."

Callie heard Tom swear under his breath, but she couldn't stop. She had to keep talking, the story tumbling out of her. "I was too afraid to pound on the door to get someone's attention. A janitor finally found me later that afternoon. I never told my family about any of the bullying incidents. They thought I was having a great time in school and I didn't have the heart to disappoint them by telling them otherwise. To this day, I still freak out in tiny, enclosed spaces. Dumb, I know."

"Not dumb at all," Tom quietly said. "So that's why you feel so strongly about bullying."

Callie nodded.

Tom reached out to cup her cheek. "I wish I'd been there to kick their butts."

"That's what you did at the square dance. In a way. You came in with some pretty girl in a blue dress. I was standing in the corner. Some local kids were making fun of me. And you told them to knock it off. You don't remember, do you? Of course you don't. It wasn't a big deal to you. But it was to me at the time. I was a couple of years younger than you were. Tex was there with me, but she'd gone to speak to your grandfather about something, so she didn't see what was going on. But you did and you stuck up for me. I didn't put things together until just now. Maybe that's when I first…"

"First what?"

Fell in love with you. The words hit her like the lightning bolt that had forced her to move in with him.

Or maybe she'd fallen in love with him when he'd been so kind to Quentin. Or when he'd kissed her after mistaking her for a stripper that very first night. Or when she'd heard his laugh. Or seen his eyes.

She loved him. The signs had been there all along, but she'd been too scared to see them.

Telling him the truth about her past had opened up a logjam of emotions. She'd shared things she'd never revealed to anyone else.

"Are you okay?" Tom asked.

"I don't know." Her voice was unsteady.

"Come here." His words rumbled together as he tugged her into his arms.

The moment their bodies met, passion took over. His lips covered hers—gently at first then hungrily—in a mating of tangled tongues that unleashed an overwhelming desire to savor more of their tempting stimulation.

Somehow, she found herself horizontal on the couch with him pressed against her. With blissful ability, his hands and lips aroused her to a pitch of unbearable excitement. He was both deliciously demanding and exquisitely tender.

She lacked his experience, but some sixth sense told her how to move, where to touch him, what to do. Tom murmured his approval and responded by slipping his hand beneath her tank top to cup her breast in the palm of his hand. He flicked open her front-fastening bra with ease.

Her nipples tightened at the prospect of his touch. His hand closed over her warm and willing flesh before brushing his thumb over one rosy peak.

The pleasure he was creating was unlike anything she'd ever experienced before.

She wanted to be even closer to him, so she slipped her hands beneath his T-shirt to caress the bare skin of his back and broad shoulders. He was hot to her touch. Her fingers rested bewitchingly on the waistband of his shorts.

She'd shared her secrets with him. Now she wanted to share *everything* with him. She loved this man. She wanted to kiss every scar and heal every wound.

But he kept distracting her as his hands made themselves familiar with every part of her—every line, every curve. She could feel his body harden against her, making her ache to have him join with her.

His mouth descended to bestow a trail of erotic kisses across her breasts until his lips closed around her, his tongue bathing her nipple. Shards of fiery delight shot through her, curving her back as she arched off the couch and further into his heated embrace.

Things rapidly moved to a new plateau of pleasure marked by breathless moans and sensuous strokes. She explored the fascinating formation of his spine. He moved his hand up her inner thigh to draw enticing erotic circles beneath the hem of her cutoffs.

His touch evoked an intimacy that was beyond temptation. The center of her being was melting like wax in a flame. She felt the evidence of his arousal and was consumed by need.

The time had come. Another crossroads. Another decision made.

When he lifted his head to kiss her again, she whispered her intentions against his lips. "Make love to me."

He released her with jarring suddenness, severing all contact.

Confused, Callie murmured her protest and reached for him, questioning his right to deprive her of his kisses.

Then he said the word that broke her heart...

Chapter Eleven

"No!"

One word. So powerful. A punch right through her heart. But there was more to come.

"I'm sorry," Tom continued as he put as much distance between them as possible. By this time, he was standing in front of the fireplace. "I can't do this."

"What do you mean?" Had his injuries prevented him from making love? "Physically, you're not able to…?"

"Oh, I'm able to, all right. But I'm not going to. I shouldn't have kissed you. It was a mistake. I was just trying to comfort you. But then things got out of hand."

"Comfort me?"

He nodded stiffly.

She was having trouble comprehending what he was telling her. "But you wanted me."

He shrugged. "You're a beautiful woman. Any man would want you. That doesn't mean anything."

Any lingering hope she may have still had was now crushed.

The hurt and humiliation was beyond bearing.

Her outward appearance may have changed, but in that moment, she once again felt like the big loser that the other kids in tenth grade had always accused her of being.

There was no way to make a dignified retreat from this mess, so she didn't even try. Instead, she flew off the couch and into the relative sanctuary of the spare bedroom, slamming and locking the door behind her.

Callie sank into the bed and buried her face in her shaking hands. How could she have been such an idiot? When would she learn? He'd told her time and time again that he wasn't interested, but she'd kept pushing, kept hoping.

His words replayed in her head. Wanting her didn't mean anything. *She* didn't mean anything to him.

So much for having faith in happy endings. She'd been right all along. They weren't meant for her.

On the other side of the locked door, Tom told himself again that he'd done the right thing. Needing some air and some distance, he left the cabin and Callie. They could both use some time to get over what had nearly happened.

But when he returned to the cabin a few hours later, it was to find the spare bedroom vacant.

Callie had left. And taken her monster cat with her.

"What did you do?" Striker growled the next morning as he stood on the front porch of the cabin.

Tom squinted at him. He hadn't gotten any sleep last night worrying about Callie.

"Do not yell at your brother," Wanda reprimanded as

she moved around Striker and entered the cabin. She looked incredibly cheerful in her purple pants and pink T-shirt with the saying Growing Old Is Mandatory, Growing Up Is Optional. "Do not worry, Thomas." She patted his cheek like she had when he was a kid. "I am here to make things better. Look, I even brought some *kolachkis*." She waved the plate full of baked goodies under his nose. "I will make some coffee and we will talk."

"You want to talk?" Striker marched into the room and glared at Tom, who glared right back. "Tex called me this morning threatening to quit because my slime-ball brother broke her granddaughter's heart. What do you have to say about that?"

"Nothing," Tom growled.

"You don't think Callie deserves better?"

"Affirmative." Tom's voice was harsh. "She does deserve better. That's the whole point."

"Explain." Striker barked the order.

Tom responded by telling Striker what he could do with himself.

"Now boys," Wanda said with a shake of her head. "Arguing will not solve anything."

"There's nothing *to* solve," Tom said curtly.

"If you two don't behave, I will call your mother," Wanda warned them both. "She's still up at the ranch house. I don't think you want her coming out here."

Tom loved his mom, but he was no fool. Angela Kozlowski might look like a sweetheart, but she had a spine of steel and an iron will. If she got word of any of this, there would be a "situation." One that they'd regret.

Striker appeared equally cautious. "There's no need for that."

"I'm glad to hear it. Now why don't you go over to the other cabin and check on the damages," Wanda told Striker.

"I did that the other day."

She gave him a look with those intense blue eyes of hers and Striker relented. "Okay, but I'll be back."

Once he'd gone, Wanda patted Tom's arm and led him to the couch. "Now then, let's talk. Here, eat a *kolachki* first." She practically stuffed it in his mouth.

While he ate, she made some instant coffee in the kitchen and brought it to him. "You look like you need this." She handed him the mug. "Did you get any sleep last night?"

"Not much."

"Because?"

Something about the way she said it made him stupidly reply, "I did not make love to Callie."

"Why not?" Wanda asked.

Tom blinked in shock.

"I know I told you that you should be married first," Wanda continued, "but I don't think that's what stopped you. So why? She loves you. You love her."

"She deserves better. Not someone who may never be able to pick her up and carry her across the threshold. She left me a note, you know. Said she wouldn't bother me ever again."

"But you liked her bothering you."

Tom said nothing. He wasn't going to lie and deny it. And there was no point in agreeing. His feelings didn't matter. He didn't matter. Callie did.

He repositioned his knee with a grimace. He'd overdone it again, trying to physically run away from his thoughts, from his reality.

Wanda sighed and joined him on the couch. "There

is a Polish saying. 'Wherever you go, you can't get rid of yourself.' You must first find peace within yourself before you can find happiness."

Peace? Tom doubted he'd ever find it. Certainly not now.

Tom had pushed Callie away because, even though she may have been a geek as a kid, she was a beauty now. He, however, was still the beast, with weaknesses and plenty of scars.

She deserved better than him.

And while she'd bared her soul and opened up to him, he was unable to do the same. He couldn't bare his soul and let her know how he really felt. He couldn't let anyone know.

During his officer training, he'd been given scenarios where he couldn't win, where there could be no positive outcome.

This felt like one of those situations. One where it was impossible to avoid failure.

Which was the point. Those tests had been designed to test his resolve. Because the last thing the Marine Corps needed in battle was a leader who was a quitter.

The point was to keep going. To keep striving.

He'd done that. Kept going. Kept striving to return to the man he'd been before.

But he wasn't stupid. Striving didn't mean that he'd ever be any more physically adept than he was now. This might be as good as he got. And that realization had been like a fist in his gut.

During his sleepless night, Tom realized he'd probably actually fallen for Callie the first moment he'd seen her—even though he'd tried very hard to fight it ever since then.

But his feelings didn't matter. The bottom line was

that she deserved the perfect man. He didn't even come close.

"There is so much darkness inside of you." Wanda cupped his face with her wrinkled hand. "Let it go, my Thomas. Know that you are worthy of coming back into the sunshine. You can't keep trying to hide these things inside." She moved her hand to his heart. "Because wherever you go, you can't get rid of yourself."

Tom clenched his jaw. But he couldn't speak.

Striker had no such problem. "I'm back," he announced from the front door.

"I will leave you two boys alone," Wanda stated. "Give me the keys to your vehicle," she ordered Striker.

To Tom's surprise, Striker obeyed.

"You let her drive your pickup truck?" Tom said.

Striker shrugged. "She's riding on the back of a motorcycle at home in Chicago. Or so I'm told."

"Busha is one of a kind."

"Yeah, she is."

Striker pulled up a chair and straddled it backward. "I did some thinking outside and I have one question. What exactly did you mean when you said that Callie deserves better?"

"Exactly what I said. She deserves better than me."

"She can't do any better than you," Striker stated emphatically and without hesitation.

"A minute ago, I was a slimeball."

"Those were Tex's words, not mine. Come on, bro. Talk to me. What's going on here?"

"I'm not the Marine I used to be." Tom's voice was rough with emotion and frustration as he pounded his clenched fist on his thigh. "I'm not the man I used to be. And don't tell me there are guys far worse off than me. Don't you think I realize that?"

Striker's gaze was filled with unexpected empathy. "When you're ambushed, you have to do the thing you least want to. You have to turn into the ambush and fight. The same thing is true in this case. You have to turn into the fear and fight it," Striker said. "To remember that courage isn't the absence of fear but the strength to fight it."

Only then did Tom realize that maybe he'd been surrendering instead of living. Taking cover instead of fighting back.

Justice had tried to tell him that, reminding him that in war planning you have to be open to new options because the conditions change all the time.

"You were ambushed not once but twice," Striker continued. "Once in that explosion that injured you over there. And again when you tried to come to terms with the aftereffects. We're Marines. We don't talk about this stuff. We don't admit to any of it. We slam the hatch shut on any hint of emotional conflict. Usually works pretty darn well. But in this case, that skunk just ain't gonna mate. You met Justice the other night. And before you ask, no, I didn't ask him to talk to you. He did that on his own. But he's been there—where you're at, dealing with those demons. And he's no loser. He has a wife and a daughter who love him. It's true, you're not the Marine you were, not the man you were. But who says you can't be even better than you were? Okay, so you might not set any speed records in a foot race, but you have brains and you have guts. That's what makes a good Marine."

Tom sat there, a little stunned at his lightbulb moment of enlightenment.

Despite all his internal claims that he was fighting to regain his former self, he'd really been grieving for what he'd lost. Enough already. He needed to focus on what he had.

Justice was right. There were still ways Tom could contribute to the Marine Corps. He wasn't a failure as a man or as a Marine.

So his future might not be the way he'd pictured it. That doesn't mean he should throw in the towel or keep chasing after impossible pipe dreams.

"I have another question for you," Striker said. "Do you love Callie?"

Tom had known the answer to that question for a while now. That had never been the problem. Despite his attempts to convince himself that he was only "in want" with her, the truth was that he loved her. Like so many of the men in his family, he'd fallen at first sight, even though he'd fought it. "Affirmative. She's the one."

"So what are you going to do about it?" Striker asked.

"I am here to help with that," Wanda stated from the doorway. At their startled looks, she added, "Your vehicle is too large for me, Striker. And you're needed at home. Your cellphone was on the front seat. Your wife appears to be going into labor."

An instant later, Striker was gone.

"Don't you want to go with him?" Tom asked Wanda.

She shook her head. "No, you need me more. You are looking better now. Must be my *kolachkis,* hmm? And my good advice, yes?"

Tom had to smile at her cheerful expression. He really did have a lot of blessings to count, and his grandmother was one of them. "That's right, Busha."

"I hooked up your twin brother with the woman meant for him, yet I have done little to help you. It's only fair that I do so now when you need me most."

"I think I can handle this on my own."

"You have not been doing such a super job on your own."

Tom had to admit that she had a point.

"That mean grandmother of Callie's is probably filling her head with stories about how bad you are," Wanda added.

"Tex doesn't really have to do that. Callie already thinks I'm pond scum." And he couldn't blame her.

"Then you have a lot of work to do."

"I realize that."

"So what is your plan?"

"To find her."

Wanda lifted one eyebrow. "And then?"

"Talk to her."

"And say what?"

"I don't know."

"Not the right answer."

Since Tom was the one who hurt Callie by sending her away, he had to go after her and try to make amends. He didn't realize he'd said the words aloud until Wanda said, "I agree. You are the one who must make amends. And I can help. I happen to know that there is a Sunday benefit later today where Callie will make an appearance."

"Doing my recon work for me now, are you, Busha?"

She grinned. "Sometimes it takes a woman to lead a man in the right direction."

"Another Polish saying of yours?"

Wanda's smile widened. "No, this one I learned all on my own."

Callie stared at her reflection in her car's rearview mirror. The eyedrops she'd used earlier had removed most of the redness as promised. She no longer looked like a woman who'd cried her eyes out most of the night, for which she was infinitely grateful.

When she'd shown up on Tex's doorstep last night, her grandmother had taken her in. Taken Bob in, too.

"I have allergy pills," Tex had assured her. "Don't you worry one bit about me."

Her grandmother had made her favorite pancakes and a mug of hot cocoa, despite the fact that it was eighty degrees outside. Callie had given Bob a dish of his favorite gourmet cat food. The comfort food had worked better for her cat than the pancakes had for her.

She was still painfully ashamed of the way she had offered herself to Tom, only to have him reject her. She'd taken a huge risk, opening herself up to him, letting him get to know the "real" Callie. The one who felt like she'd gone through those years with a giant *L* for loser branded in the middle of her freckled forehead.

The freckles had faded a bit. So had the burning humiliation of those years. Until last night. She'd shared some of her deepest secrets with Tom. But when she'd wanted to share everything with him, he'd pushed her away.

She'd bounced back before when he'd told her that he wasn't interested in a relationship with her.

She'd even bounced back when he'd said that kissing her was a "mistake."

But Callie didn't think she'd ever bounce back from this last rejection.

She'd read someplace once that you never see yourself the way the world sees you. That the truth inside your head is formed by those images of your youth and differs from the truth everyone else sees.

Whatever "truth" Tom had seen in her, he hadn't been interested.

She had to get over it. Get over him.

It wasn't going to happen in a day.

But she was a pro at hiding her inner turmoil and putting on a happy face. She'd done it for her family throughout her school years. She'd wanted to please them when they'd been so determined that she go to St. Mary's Academy. They'd been so proud of her getting that scholarship.

Her cellphone rang and a glance down at the screen told her it was her dad. "Hey, honey," he said with his customary cheerfulness. "How are you doin'?"

"I'm fine."

"That's not what your grandma says."

"You know how Gran is."

"Want me to come up there and give that Marine a verbal whoopin'?"

"No. Don't worry about me."

"I do worry. I realize I haven't called you as much as I should have the past few weeks...."

"That's okay."

"No, it's not. I got caught up in this new reorganization thing at work, but you always come first with me. I hope you know that, honey."

"I know." For a second, she was tempted to finally tell her dad about those awful days in school. But what would be the point? He'd only feel bad for not knowing about it at the time, for not protecting her. She knew him well enough to know that. No, there was no point in telling him or Gran about it now. That was all water under the bridge.

And, yes, it still came back to haunt her sometimes. But she'd made huge strides since those days. She was an outstanding teacher. She had great friends like Paula. She was a force to be reckoned with.

But just because she was confident about some things, that didn't mean that she didn't still have scars. And that was okay. Plenty of people had scars. Some spent years in therapy to get over them. Some resorted to drugs or alcohol or other addictions.

If the worst thing she did was make an idiot of herself over Tom, then she wasn't doing too badly.

Or so she firmly informed her reflection, before ending the call with her dad and getting out of her car.

The picnic basket auction today was intended to raise money for the literacy program at the public library that was so dear to Callie's heart. It looked like they already had a good crowd gathered.

The weather report had promised another beautiful day, hot and sunny. As always, she'd applied plenty of sunscreen, and the outfit she was wearing—a swirly little floral skirt and a sleeveless lilac top—was intended to be a morale booster.

The park where the event was taking place was filled with colorful balloons and people of all ages. She recognized some of the kids from her class, including Adam and Anna and their families. Many of the participants from the literacy program, like José and Rosaria, were there, as well.

Booths had been set up for fun activities like face painting. Watching the kids getting half moons and stars drawn on their cheeks reminded Callie of that last day of school when Tom had shown up in his dress blues and she'd teased him about avoiding face painting.

A gentle wind fluttered through the live oaks that edged the park, cooling Callie's heated face. Her heart ached. Actually ached. Luckily, she had no tears left.

The last thing she needed today was a reminder of a certain Marine.

So naturally, that's what fate threw her way. First with the face painting, then with someone wearing a *Star Wars* T-shirt, then with a man playing an accordion.

The final straw was provided by Quentin, who was there with his mom and eagerly approached Callie to ask, "Is Captain Tom coming today?"

"No," Callie replied, her body tensing at yet another reminder of the man she'd fallen so stupidly and so deeply in love with.

Glancing down at Quentin's crestfallen face, she realized her curt reply had thrown him. "No, he can't be here today," she said, more gently this time.

"I'm sorry to hear that," Quentin's mom said. "I'm so grateful for all he's done for my son. I just wanted to thank him again. Can you do that the next time you see him?"

Callie just nodded. It was easier than explaining that she had no intention of ever seeing Tom again.

"Hey, you," Paula greeted her a few minutes later. "How's your summer going so far?"

"Don't ask."

"Oh no. That doesn't sound good at all. Did something go wrong between you and your Marine?"

It occurred to Callie that the very first time she'd talked to Paula about Tom she admitted that she'd made an idiot of herself. What a precursor for what was to come.

"Forget about it." Callie deliberately put a big smile on her face and linked her arm with her friend's. "Let's focus on the event today. I'm so happy to see such a big crowd here for the picnic basket auction."

"Me, too. I told my husband he'd better bid on my basket or else."

"I doubt he needed much arm twisting since the winning bidder not only gets your picnic lunch but also gets to eat it with you."

Callie accompanied Paula to the receiving area, where they handed over their picnic baskets to the person in charge. An auctioneer had volunteered her time to oversee the actual bidding, which started a few minutes later.

Callie was pleased to see so many baskets going for good prices. She wished hers would come up soon. She was getting a little nervous wondering if anyone would bid on it at all.

She knew her insecurities were a residual from the events of last night. Knowing didn't make them disappear, however.

Finally, her basket came up. As was the protocol, she went to the front of the crowd and stood beside the auctioneer. "Our next item is a lovely picnic basket created by Callie Murphy."

Her grandmother hooted and hollered from the back of the crowd, sounding loud enough for a party of five all by herself.

"What goodies do you have inside your picnic basket?" the auctioneer asked Callie.

"Homemade fried chicken," Callie replied. Tex had actually provided the chicken since Callie had been too distraught to do that. "And potato salad, also homemade. Oh, and chocolate chip cookies made from scratch." She'd baked those herself in the middle of the night.

"Sounds great. We'll begin the bidding at ten dollars."

Tex raised her hand. "I bid ten dollars."

"Great. We have an opening bid of ten dollars. How about fifteen?"

"I bid fifteen," came a male voice from the other side of the crowd.

"Great. We have a bid for fifteen—"

"Fifteen *thousand* dollars."

The crowd gasped and then parted like the Red Sea as a Marine in dress blues slowly made his way toward the front.

Callie was stunned.

What was he doing? Trying to make up for a guilty conscience because he'd hurt her feelings last night?

"Sir, did you say fifteen *thousand* dollars was your bid?"

"Affirmative." Tom kept his eyes on Callie as if willing her to look at him. But after one quick glance, she kept her gaze averted. He was using his cane. Did that mean his leg was worse today?

"Sold!" The auctioneer quickly banged her gavel as if she was afraid Tom would have second thoughts and retract his bid.

"No, I…" Callie sputtered. But it was too late to protest. Instead of worrying about his leg, she should have been withdrawing her basket from the auction. But that would have meant losing fifteen thousand dollars for the literacy fund-raiser. No way she could have done that.

She was stuck with him. That didn't mean she had to be happy about it, though.

She grabbed her basket and marched off. Tom followed her. His pace may have been slower than hers, but his face reflected his determination.

To do what, she wasn't sure.

When they'd reached a relatively uncrowded area of the park, she headed for an empty picnic bench and set her basket on it with a decided thump before pivoting to face him. "Look, I don't know what you're up to, but you're crazier than a lizard with sunstroke if you think—"

"I think I've fallen in love with a sassy redhead and I'm here to tell her so," Tom stated.

Callie's mouth gaped open. She sputtered for a moment before the ability to form words returned. "You are certifiable!"

"Probably," Tom agreed.

She narrowed her eyes at him. "Is this some kind of sick joke?"

"If so, then the laugh is on me."

"You pushed me away last night."

"The most difficult thing I've ever done in my life." He looked grave and tired. His eyes were dark, filled with emotions and experiences she could only guess at.

In the past, his tough facade would only crack for a moment or two, giving her fleeting glimpses of what really made him tick. Just enough to tantalize her, to get to her but not enough to share with her.

Now she saw for the first time the torment he'd gone through. Because for the first time, he *allowed* her to see. He'd let his defenses down. A huge thing for a man like Tom.

But was it all an act? Was this his way of drawing her back in so that he could kick her in the teeth again?

"I had to push you away for your own good," he continued. "Because you deserved better. At least, that's what I thought. You have to understand, I'd always considered myself to be a perfect Marine, stronger and better than most. Until that ambush. It changed everything for me. Left me feeling incompetent and like less of a man. But there were plenty of guys worse off than I was, so I had no right to feel that way. Or so I told myself. I should've just sucked it up and moved on. But I didn't know who I was anymore."

Her heart ached for him, making her want to reach out and put her arms around him. But the pain of his recent rejection was still too powerful. "And now you do know who you are?"

"I am a Marine. One who can't move as fast but one who fights for what he believes in. And I believe in you and me. In us."

"But you didn't believe last night?"

"My feelings for you didn't matter. Like I said before, doing what was best for *you* mattered."

Anger coursed through her. "Do you have any idea how arrogant it is to think that you know what's best for me?"

"I was trying to do the right thing. My goal was to make you happy."

"By rejecting me? After I'd just bared my soul to you?"

"By not saddling you with a man who may never be able to walk normally," he retorted. "And there's also the matter of my swearing to Tex that your reputation was safe with me, that I wouldn't seduce you."

"You didn't. I was trying to seduce you, not that I succeeded."

"You succeeded the second you walked into my cabin for the very first time."

Callie was afraid to believe him.

He could read that on her face. "How can I convince you?"

They were interrupted by the arrival of the accordion player, who started serenading them.

"We're trying to have a conversation here," Tom curtly told him.

"Your grandmother sent me over to play something romantic for you two," the musician replied.

And then it hit Callie. "You just asked me how you could prove it to me. Play the accordion."

"What did you want me to play?" the musician asked with an eager expression.

"Not you. Him." Callie pointed to Tom. "You told me that you could play the accordion. Well then, play it."

By now, a small crowd had started to gather.

"Now Callie—" Tom began.

"Prove it," she said, her eyes daring him.

Remembering the pain in her eyes last night, he figured she deserved her pound of his flesh, especially if it made his case to her.

Two minutes later, he had the accordion strapped over his shoulders and resting on his chest. "I may be a little rusty…." he warned.

Rusty was an understatement. He played some kind of polka, his fingers awkwardly moving over the keys, making the instrument's owner wince and several onlookers cover their ears.

"Satisfied?" Tom asked once he was done.

"You could use lessons," the accordion's owner told him as he quickly took his instrument back.

"Yes, you could," Callie agreed, blinking back tears.

"Was I that bad that you have to cry?" he teased her.

She shook her head. "You need to learn to stop making assumptions about me, thinking you know what's right for me."

"I know a good teacher," Tom said with a hopeful smile.

"So do I. First off, don't you ever think that you're saddling me with anything but the incredibly courageous and awesome man that you are," she said fiercely.

"Understood?" She jabbed his chest with her index finger.

He gently took her hand in his and kissed the back of her fingers. "Yes, ma'am. I love you," Tom told her. "If you'll just give me another chance—"

Callie placed the fingers of her free hand on his lips. The man had played the accordion for her. In front of others. What more did she want? Only him. That's all she'd wanted all along. Just him. "I love you, too."

"Enough to marry me?"

Callie nodded, tears of happiness overflowing.

"You no-good son of a sea dog," the newly arrived Tex growled from the gathering crowd, marching forward to confront them. "You made my granddaughter cry!"

"I just asked her to be my wife," Tom said.

"And I said yes," Callie added.

"Well, it sure took you two long enough," Tex noted, her smile as big as the state of Texas. "Anyone with the IQ of a cantaloupe could see you two were in love."

"I agree," Wanda said as she joined them. "But I have more good news to share. Kate has had a baby girl, seven pounds ten ounces. Both Mom and Baby are doing fine."

"Whooee," Tex exclaimed with a big grin and a high five to Wanda.

As their grandmothers hugged each other, Tom looked down at Callie as he tugged her into his arms.

"Are you sure about this?" he asked her.

"Lesson number one, never doubt what your teacher tells you. And, yes, I'm sure," she said with a big smile. "Downright positive. Sure as shootin'. A guaranteed fact...."

"You Texans talk too much," Tom murmured before lowering his head and kissing her while the crowd around them cheered.

Epilogue

Two months later...

"There's nothing quite like a Marine wedding in dress blues," Striker stated.

"You should know," Tom retorted. "We've had enough of them in this family."

"I eloped," Steve reminded his twin.

"I'm starting to wish I had, too," Tom muttered.

"Bite your tongue," his mother told him. "I can't believe we got the entire family together in such a short time."

"She's just happy to see all her kids," Striker noted with a grin.

"And grandkids," Ben added, his sleeping baby daughter's cheek resting on his shoulder.

"Yeah, and grandkids. I can't believe both our wives had their kids at the same time, down to the minute. Although my baby girl weighed more," Striker pointed out.

"By an ounce," Ben scoffed.

"Competitive to the end," their mom sighed.

"So my wedding is just an excuse for all of you to get together, is that it?" Tom demanded.

"Works for me," Steve noted. "By the way, did I happen to mention that my wife is pregnant?"

"So is mine," Rad said.

"With twins?" Steve countered.

"No way!"

Steve nodded.

Tom thumped his twin on the shoulder, the Marine equivalent of a hug. Steve had told him the news earlier, but he was still thrilled for him. Then he thumped his brother Rad to congratulate him, too.

"Okay, enough of this baby talk," Tom stated decisively. "I have a wedding to secure here. We need to concentrate on the mission at hand. Steve, your position is best man. Do you have the ring?"

Steve nodded. "Check."

"Everyone know their assignments?" Tom demanded.

"We're Marines, son." His dad laid a reassuring hand on his shoulder. "We have the situation totally under control."

"I hate to think of losing my little girl," Callie's dad said in a husky voice when it was just the two of them waiting for that special walk down the aisle together.

"You're not losing me. You're gaining a son. A Marine. Well, actually you're gaining an entire family of Marines," she noted with a grin. "The Kozlowskis are a tight-knit family, as you may have noticed."

"Yeah, I got that impression."

The music started. Callie grinned at the sound of the opening notes of the *Star Wars* theme, which was soon followed by the much more traditional "Wedding March."

"I love you, honey," her dad said. "Are you ready?" He kissed her cheek and offered her his arm.

"I'm ready," Callie replied without hesitation.

The church was filled with people important to Callie and Tom. Marines and teachers. Students and friends. And, most importantly, family.

As she walked down the aisle toward the love of her life, Callie knew she'd found her dream Marine.

As Tom watched her come closer, he knew he'd found the one woman meant for him.

They were, indeed, soul mates.

The ceremony went without a hitch right up until the minister said, "You may kiss—"

Tom didn't wait for him to finish before gathering Callie in his arms. She laughed with delight at his eagerness and looped her arms around his neck with equal enthusiasm. The church erupted with Marines calling out "Ooh-rah!" as Tom kissed his new bride with a passionate devotion that had all the women in the crowd sighing and fanning themselves.

And in the front pew, Wanda sent up a special Polish prayer, thankful that all her dreams for her tough Marine grandsons had finally come true. They'd each found the most precious thing of all—true love.

* * * * *

COMING NEXT MONTH

#1806 A TAIL OF LOVE—Alice Sharpe
PerPETually Yours

Marnie is a wire fox terrier with a mission: reunite his family.
With strategically placed canine chaos as his main tool, if he can get
the career-focused Rick Manning and the easygoing teacher Isabelle
Winters back together, he just might prove that dog is a *couple's*
best friend....

#1807 IN GOOD COMPANY—Teresa Southwick
Buy-a-Guy

A newly svelte Molly Preston has something to prove. And
"buying" former big man on campus Des O'Donnell as her date
for their high school reunion will go a long way toward righting
old wrongs. Or will it? Because not "winning" Des's love now
seems a far greater wrong.

#1808 SNOW WHITE BRIDE—Carol Grace
Fairy-Tale Brides

When Sabrina White runs away from her own wedding and arrives
on his doorstep in a blinding snowstorm, Zach Prescott's seven
nieces and nephews mistake her for Snow White. And though
Zach doesn't believe in fairy tales, this tycoon can't deny his
young charges a happy ending....

#1809 THE MATCHMAKING MACHINE—
Judith McWilliams

Loyal to her fired coworker, Maggie Romer seethes for revenge
upon the new boss, Richard Worthington. Writing a computer
program that analyzes Richard's preference in women, Maggie
wants to become her, seduce him and dump him! That is, until his
kisses show her that sometimes the best-laid plans of women and
machines can go deliciously awry!

SRCNM0206